# THE LURE OF FIRE

## CHLOE O'CONNOR

# THE LURE
# OF FIRE

The Elemental Series
Book One

By Chloe O'Connor

*Lauren,*
*If it wasn't for you and your love of fantasy, I don't know*
*how I would have gotten through this story without you.*
*This one is for you.*

# Content Guidance

AMAROK
ARCHURILLIA
Academy of Elements
Rimemoud
FIRE COURT
PHOENIX
EARTH COURT
Clearhill
OUROBOROS
AIR COURT
Flossmau
SERPANT
N
W
E
S
Ebonwater
WATER COURT
Baysummit
REALM OF INIXIAM
GRIFFIN

# Chapter One

"Can you believe we are finally here?" Aylee's voice is filled with awe and anticipation. I look ahead at the giant black gates in front of me, and all I feel is dread and the anxiety creeping up my spine. I knew this day would come when we had to enroll into the Academy of Elements, but who can put off turning twenty-one? I sure couldn't.

The Academy has been around for nearly the same amount of time as the war we are in with the humans and their forbidden creatures. The humans hate us, they believe having powers and the ability to use magic is corrupt and forbidden. The Fae gathered a council of the strongest among them to create a hierarchy of our land. *The Lords*. They will be the ones to oversee their own ability court and to have a peace treaty with each elemental court. The humans, on the other hand, worked out a way to harness that magic but since they weren't born with the ability, it all went wrong.

Some humans are at peace with it all, but they are in

hiding and they even bred with Fae. Although it is frowned upon from both sides of the war, but some just don't care.

For centuries, every warrior who has been fighting in this war have been to this Academy. This is the place where you either become something or you can die trying. Or the worst case, return home and become nobody but a failure.

"I wish we weren't," I mutter to myself. I'm not exactly jumping for joy to be here, but this is my one step closer to possibly seeing my brother, who attended the Academy a few years ago. Although, the thought of myself stronger for the impending war that's plagued these lands for thousands of years is appealing.

"Don't be like that, Ash, you know these next six months will turn us into badass warriors, who could be chosen for the front lines against the Nurrigorgen and the awful creatures they command." Aylee turns to me and raises her blond eyebrows and cocks her head to the side.

"Plus, I'm sure there'll be some cute boys here to mess around with too." She nudges my shoulder in a playful manner.

"That doesn't convince me at all." Our entire lives we were taught simple magic use by our parents, and now we get shipped off to a school where we get to learn so much more. It's a test to wean out the weak. No one wants a weak Fae to command the front lines against the evil creature, Crowid, and die within seconds. No, they want warriors to be strong and cunning against them so we can stand a chance.

That's why we have been sent here today.

"Come on, we have to mark our presence." Aylee grabs my hand, and we walk right into the gates. The brown pavement is smooth under my shoes, the flow of my blue-and-gold dress sways in the wind, and my loose hair laps around my face.

The second we pass through the gates, I feel the energy surge through my entire being, it's the wards surrounding the Academy.

It alerts the authorities if a student has snuck off the grounds and to protect us from the evil lurking beyond the borders.

The creatures don't dare do anything out in broad daylight, and they aren't as clever as they have been portrayed. I roll my eyes when I catch Aylee glancing in the direction of five or so guys standing by the entrance to the hall.

"Come on, let's introduce ourselves... I think one of them is staring at you, Ash." Aylee tugs my hand, and my feet carry me to the destination of the group of guys.

"Hey! I'm Aylee and this is my best friend Aisling." I watch in dread as Aylee introduces us. I don't want to be here, I just wanted to keep a low profile for the next six months. Then earn my badge and march my way to the front lines, where my brother is stationed. I haven't seen Alec in three years. I miss him.

"It's nice to meet you." One of the guys steps forward and outstretches his hand. Aylee takes it, I turn away and see the teachers make their way to the podium. The introductions are about to start, and all Aylee is concerned about is getting laid later.

"Come on, let's go," I lean over and say quietly to her.

"You won't miss much; they just talk about how to behave and to earn top marks in your classes. It's rather boring." A male voice comes from the back of the group. He steps forward and I try to blink back how gorgeous he is.

How is looking like that legal?

"How would you know?" I snap.

"My brother told me everything from last year, and my oldest brother before him. It's the same speech, year after year." He smirks down at me.

He's maybe six foot three compared to my five foot five.

"Well, I don't trust your brothers." I tilt my chin up to challenge him. I watch as he lifts his right hand and strokes his golden blond hair back off his tanned forehead.

"Feisty little thing, aren't you?" He tilts his head to look me up and down. I can't help but fidget my hands on the gold rope tied at my waist to keep my dress tight against my hips.

I've never found myself attractive, with my mousy brown hair and violet eyes. I'm nothing compared to Aylee, who's blond hair is tied back into a braid crown on the top of her head, her green eyes always sparkling because she's always in a good mood, and her figure has more curves than I can count. She's a walking dream for any man.

"You have no idea." Aylee laughs and jabs an elbow into my waist.

"What element can you wield?" One of the smaller guys steps around the others, asking Aylee and completely ignoring me.

"I'm from Earth Court." She does a quick twirl and the small rocks from the ground float up and around her. She's giving them a show, I roll my eyes at her. Of course, she does something like this.

"What about you, Feisty?" The tall guy standing in front and center asks me, his dark eyes narrowing in on mine, challenging me.

"Water." I look back at him with the same intensity, hoping he is the first one to break contact.

"She's incredible," Aylee says beside me.

I'm the one who breaks contact first.

"I'm okay." I shrug, not wanting to give them any indication I am more than okay with my magic, but they don't have to know that... yet.

"Same here." He smirks, but yet I haven't seen him anywhere in Water Court. I should know, my father used to be the right-hand man to the Lord. Lord Marcus.

"I haven't seen you." Confusion is evident on my face.

"I've lived in the war camps my entire life; my father is the general. So, I never got to visit *our* Court." The way he says the word *our* is like it should mean something, like we share something.

We don't.

"Come on, Aylee, I want to listen." I smirk at this enchanting male in front of me. I don't want to give in to his temptation.

Aylee and I walk, arms linked, and leave behind *the* challenge I'll face in these next six months.

# Chapter Two

"I can't believe we got the same room!" Aylee shrieks when we were handed our room information.

"I can't believe it either!" I do though, I put in a room request at the start of the year, I knew I couldn't get by these six months without her, but I'll never tell her that. Her ego is already sky-high as it is.

"Hey." A small mousy voice comes from the propped open bedroom door.

Aylee and I both turn around and inspect who it is.

"I'm in this room," she says.

"Yay, welcome. I'm Aylee and this is my best friend, Aisling." Aylee extends her hand, and the new member of our room takes it.

She's hesitant but takes it.

"I'm Neeshah." She smiles shyly. You wouldn't think she was this small shy girl, but she's close to six feet tall, long orange hair—almost like hot flames wrapped around her shoulders—and bright amber eyes. Her complexion is golden brown and somehow her skin shimmers in the sunlight. She's stunning.

"I'm from Earth Court, Ash is from Water and I'm guessing by your eyes you're from Fire Court?" Aylee asks. I nudge her side; we don't always assume which court we are from. It is also more obvious though as each person's eyes represent where they are from. It does get a bit harder if parents of their own court mix and have children. Either their eyes are more predominant from their father's side, or they tend to have a mixture of the two, but that is very rare. I've never come across anyone who has a mixture of the two, as it is also rare for two Fae to stray from their own court and marry.

"Sorry," Aylee mutters.

"No, don't apologize. You aren't the first person to ask me that, but you are right. I am from Fire Court." She weakly smiles at us.

"Don't just stand there, come in. Make yourself at home... we sure have." I gesture to the room for her to step inside and she does.

"Thanks, I'm really glad I've bunked with two nice girls. I can't imagine being in someone else's room who aren't so nice... especially since I'm from Fire Court." She shrugs and takes the right bed in the room. We have three single beds all lined in a row, they are covered in plain gray sheets and at the end of the bed are our uniforms—fighting leathers.

There is a single desk in the far-right corner of the room and beside it is a bookshelf.

There is one bay window that outlooks onto the court-yard of the Academy but apart from that the entire room is completely bare.

*Knock... knock...*

I whip my head around to face our door and walk away from Aylee and Neeshah, who are in deep conversation. I wonder who would be knocking on our door.

Could it be staff handing out our class schedules?

I open the door and I'm a little surprised, but I supress it down and scowl at our guest.

"Is that how you always greet people, Fireball?" He tilts his head to the side slightly.

*Fireball...*

He's already giving me nicknames.

"I don't like strangers knocking on my door," I snidely reply back.

"It's Gerrick, and I'm just paying a courtesy call... since you'll be needing these." He smirks at me.

"Who's at the door?" Aylee calls out from behind me.

"It's no one." I smirk right back at him.

This is going to be fun.

I take the pieces of paper from his hands and close the door in his face.

My cheeks burn from the heat of his words and presence. Is it always going to be like this?

No. No, I mentally shake that thought out of my head. I can't be attracted to someone like *that*. Someone so... arrogant.

"Here, these are our class schedules." I hand both the girls their papers. I look down at mine and the first class I'm taking tomorrow is combat. I let out a long sigh. My least favorite.

* * *

"I'll see you after class." I smile at Aylee and Neesh. I can't believe they didn't get the same classes as me. I can't be completely alone for these six months.

"I'll meet you at the courtyard for lunch," Aylee calls back when her and Neesh walk toward academics. They have the same schedule, and I feel kinda left out. I guess I must make another new friend for my classes, if I want to survive these next few months.

"Sure thing," I call back out.

I look at the dark wooden door in front of me, it's old and cold to the touch. I ignore the fear building deep inside me, and I push open the door to the combat gym. I look around the room, there are four fighting mats in the middle of the room. Weights are to the left of where I stand with a large mirror spanning the entire wall. And on the other side of the room are seats and a weaponry wall.

I take note that there isn't anyone here yet, good. That will give me a few minutes to collect myself. I walk over to the weaponry wall and inspect all the weapons lining the wooden racks. I see a sword I like, and I lift it off the rack. I like how light it is, the tilt of the blade and the leather binding on the hilt, but it just doesn't feel right as I take a step back and swing it in the air. It's too long, it doesn't give me the flexibility to quickly change positions.

My brother taught my sisters and me how to wield a sword, in the hopes we would attend the Academy. Though it was our choice whether we wanted to attend or not... I wasn't keen at first, but Aylee wanted to join so I followed her. My brother didn't exactly go into depth with the combat training or the academics of this place, he thought if we had a weapon, we would be safe.

"Who would have thought you were a sword wielder, Fireball," I hear *his* voice from behind me. I let the sword hang down my arm and turn to face him.

"Gerrick," I say with little to no effort.

I take in his appearance; he's dressed like me in fighting leathers with long leather sleeves to protect our arms, a tight-fitted chest piece, mine is more a corset with how tight it is. He has tight leather pants and plain black boots. He looks amazing.

I look back into his deep blue eyes and down to his perfect lips and I see them smirk.

Fuck.

I'm staring.

"See anything you like?" he asks.

"No," I say too quickly.

He chuckles, a sound that vibrates through every nerve of my body.

"I'm sure," he barely whispers the words.

"What are you even doing here?" I ask him once I've gathered myself mentally.

"I'm here for my first class, just like you." He raises his eyebrow and leans back against the wall beside the door. He crosses his arms against his chest, so casual for him.

Great. I was hoping to avoid him.

I'm about to say something smart when the other students start filing into the room, chatting away with each other, and they are followed by our instructor, Mr. Rowenfield. I've read about him; he has been given medals for his bravery against the Nurrigorgen. They are the humans who have used their element powers for evil. They are the dangerous kind. They aren't human anymore; they've transformed into hideous beasts.

No one knows the details of what happened or why he was awarded those medals. All we know from the books and reports are that something terrible happened and, of course, those documents with the right information are classified.

"All right, ladies and gentlemen. I'm not going to sugarcoat anything this year. You will either die or survive after your training here. It's up to you how you choose your destiny." He stands in front of us and gives a whole speech about really taking everything in, but the most important class is this one.

He looks down at his notepad and calls, "The first pair to take the mat is Aisling and Gerrick." Once we step toward the mat, Mr. Rowenfield waves his hand and the air around us turns thick like smoke. I can't see anything in front of me. I can hear the other students mutter amongst themselves but some gasp in shock with the surrealness of it all.

I stand on the mat and face Gerrick. Of all the students I had to engage in my first class, it had to be him.

"Let's see what you've got, Fireball." He lifts his hand and motions his pointy finger to come toward him.

I look around the thick smoke and I can't see anything except Gerrick, I can't hear the other students in the gym. It's just the two of us alone.

Combat is the one thing I dread the most. I mean, there isn't anything wrong with combat, it's just I'm not very good at it. My older brother tried to teach me the basics before he went away to war, but I just couldn't get anything to stick. I would win a few matches but looking back at the memory now, that's probably because he let me win... I sigh.

Let's get this ass-whopping over with.

I take a step forward, and before I can get my bearings, Gerrick has landed a punch to my stomach. He could have aimed for my face, but he wanted me to lose my balance with the force, and I stumble backward and land on my ass. He steps over me with a wicked glint in his eyes, but instead of finishing me off, he offers me his hand. I stupidly take it and before I can get my bearings again, he flips me over his shoulder, and I land hard on the mat. My left side shoots with pain, exactly on my ribs, the air in my lungs leaves with a whoosh.

Fuck.

I can't catch my breath. Whatever air is left in my lungs feels like fire and heat rises in my chest, and I feel so much rage. I see *red*.

I roll to my side and quickly stand and face him again.

"I hate you," I spit the words in his direction, but he doesn't take notice as he's running at me and lands a blow to my head.

I instantly see black.

# Chapter Three

"Are you okay, Ash?" Neesh asks me once we've retired to our room.

"Yeah, just a bruised ego." I cringe, that and a massive headache with ringing in my ears. When I roll over on my side, I wince at the pain. The bed is soft, but it doesn't mask the pain I feel in my ribs and my head. I just want a redo. That was so humiliating, being carried out of the combat room to the infirmary. I was treated but told to rest the remainder of the day. I didn't even get to see who was in my other classes.

I can't believe Gerrick did that to me.

Was he trying to prove a point?

Whatever that point was.

"Are you sure? I can see if they can make you a remedy to take the pain away." Aylee comes and sits on the end of my bed.

It's sweet they want to help but I must nurse these wounds myself. They will teach me to be better. To do better.

"I'm sure. Thanks." I smile weakly at them.

"Please tell me about your classes, how were they? The teachers any good? Any interesting classmates?" I ask them both, hoping to distract me from the pain and from them hovering over me.

"Yeah, I really enjoyed Element class. I got to use some of my magic, and Mrs. Storm was really impressed with my progress so far." Aylee beamed. I knew she was a born a natural.

"Yeah, you should have seen her, Ash, she could heal plants with her power when they were practically dead!" Neesh adds.

Great, just great.

"I enjoyed Mythic 101. We got to learn about the Ancient Guardians and their power contributing to the realm," Neesh adds.

"As for interesting students, I don't think there was anyone who stood out, except that one girl who caught her desk on fire and couldn't put it out." Neeshah laughs.

"Yes! How did I completely forget about that... what was her name?" Aylee asks Neesh.

"I think it was something like Sabrina, Sarah, I don't know." Neesh shrugs.

"It was Saybie!" Aylee beams.

"Was her element fire?" I ask curiously.

"I think so, once the fire was put out, she was dismissed for the day. I would hate to be in her position." I wish I could comment more about my day, but it was over before it even began. Nothing exciting happened except getting knocked out.

"I'm sure tomorrow will be better, Ash, don't let today get you down. I wish I was there so I could have kicked Gerrick's ass myself." Aylee always has my back, but this is something I have to do myself.

*Knock... knock...*

"Who the fuck is at our door!?" I wince at the pain.

"Don't you dare move, I'll go." Neesh gets off her bed and walks to the door. She opens it enough to get a glimpse of who's on the other side, and she slams it shut just as quickly.

"Who was it?" Aylee asks.

"No one."

"Come on, let me in. I want to see her." *That* voice.

"He has some nerve," I say under my breath.

"Please," he begs behind the door.

I sigh. "Let him in." I try to sit up in bed but only manage to get halfway. Leaning against my pillow, I pull the covers up my chest to conceal my nightwear.

I hold my breath when Neesh opens the door and lets Gerrick inside. He just looks as beautiful as before. I feel the heat rise in my cheeks again.

Fuck.

I shouldn't have this response when he was the one who knocked me out in combat training.

"What do you want?" I spit the words at him.

"I brought you some food, I wasn't sure if you had eaten today after... after this morning." He shifts his feet and avoids my eyes.

Neesh takes the small basket of food from him and sets it on the desk. It smells good and on cue my stomach rumbles.

"Well, thanks for that, but you need to leave." I let out a breath of anger. He has a nerve for even being here.

"I wanted to say I am sorry, sorry for what happened and I really didn't mean it. I have a reputation to uphold here at the Academy and I wanted you to know that." He takes a step toward me, but I shift back in the bed, if that is even possible.

"Good to know, now you need to leave." I point to the door.

"Now." Neesh is walking toward him, giving him the hint that she will throw him out if necessary.

"I am sorry, Ash," he says the words just before the door slams shut in his face.

"I hate to admit it, but I am hungry." I chuckle a little.

Neesh picks the basket back up from the desk, walks to my bed, and hands it to me.

"What is his deal?" Aylee says with a hint of anger in her voice.

"I have no idea, but he is really getting on my nerves," I say around a piece of cheese and bread. It's not much, but I guess the thought is there.

"He's a piece of shit, if you ask me." Neesh gets the words out around gritted teeth.

"You don't even know him," I say, shrugging.

"Neither do you and from what I've heard from other classmates and *you*. I've made up my mind, Ash, stay away from him." She looks me dead in the eye. I think it's going to be a lot harder than that.

"I'll try, but I think you might have to tell him that."

* * *

I'm back in combat training the next day, but Mr. Rowenfield thought it was best if I sit out of today's session. Just observe the other students and take notes on what to do in my next mat session.

"That's it, good stance there, Tyike," Mr. Rowenfield says to a red-haired boy.

Sitting on a bench with two of my other classmates, I lean over to hear what they are talking about.

"Who do you think will win?" one student asks the other.

"My bet is on Gerrick."

"Nah, I heard Tyike is a lethal."

"I hope Tyike wins," I chime in.

They both look in my direction.

"Aren't you the girl who got her ass whooped by Gerrick?" one asks me.

"My name is Aisling, and yes. That was me, but it won't happen again." I tilt my chin up; I don't want to hide from the embarrassment I feel right now.

"I'm Rikie and this is my sister, Rakie." I smile at them both.

"Do you know when we will use the weapons to train?" I ask Rikie, maybe he might know the schedule. I scan the room, but I don't see *him* anywhere.

"Mr. Rowenfield told us yesterday that it will come in a few weeks' time. When everyone is ready and can hold their own on the mat." Rikie smirks at me and raises his eyebrows. He's making a point that I must be ready before picking up a sword.

Great.

I know I can hold my own with a sword, but hand-to-hand combat isn't my strength spot, and I think the entire class knows that.

The door swings open and in rushes Gerrick. I thought I had escaped him for at least one class today. He strides straight for Mr. Rowenfield, but he doesn't even look my way.

"Sorry I'm late, General Bates wanted to see me." I didn't think anyone here would get direct contact to the war front. Let alone a general. I wonder what that was about.

"Anything I should be concerned about?"

"No, sir. My father just wanted to check in..." He fidgets his fingers, interlocking with one another. This conversation is making him nervous.

Why would his father want to visit him?

That's why we have messengers, to send information out and to receive letters. This is strange, something bigger is going on and I am curious indeed.

"Very well, take the mat." My eyes follow Gerrick's back when he takes the mat and stands in front of Tyike. This time the gray mist isn't surrounding them. I wonder why Mr. Rowenfield isn't doing it.

They circle one another and then Tyike advances. He practically runs at Gerrick, but he just stands there and waits for the last second to step out of the way. It's like he knew it was coming.

Gerrick quickly spins around and punches Tyike square in the jaw, but Tyike doesn't stagger. He takes the hit with pride, and he lands one on Gerrick and that's surprising.

"Keep it clean," Mr. Rowenfield calls out to the two boys.

What even is a clean fight?

We should be learning to save ourselves in case we are invaded or for when we go to the front lines.

"You're going to pay for that," Gerrick grinds out from his locked jaw. I can see the rage in his eyes.

"That's enough. Class is over for today." He doesn't pay attention to the other students; his full focus is on these two. I have a feeling something is going to happen and it's going to be bad...very bad.

"Come on then, pretty boy. Show me what you're made of." Gerrick advances but his punch is mere millimeters away from making contact to Tyike.

"Is that your best shot?" he teases.

That's when I see it. Gerrick charges for Tyike and bowls him over, Tyike is up in the air and lands on his back and before I can inhale a sharp breath, Gerrick is on his knees and has his bare hands wrapped around Tyike's throat.

"THAT'S ENOUGH!" Mr. Rowenfield yells at them but they don't seem to hear him.

Then the entire room stops.

It's completely silent when we hear a SNAP.

Gerrick just killed Tyike.

What the fuck?

Next to me, Rakie bends over her knees and throws up her entire breakfast. I take it she's never seen death before.

I feel like doing the exact same thing, but I can't.

"Everyone out, now!" Mr. Rowenfield yells to those who stayed and watched the last mat.

I'm stuck, frozen in my spot. I can't believe I just witnessed someone die, right in front of me.

That's never happened to me before.

I've experience death of a loved one but nothing like this.

One minute they are there and the next their lifeless body is just slumped on the mat next to Gerrick.

"I..." I'm frozen, all I can feel is my pulse race under my skin. The boom, boom, boom in my ears.

When I finally inhale a breath to clear my mind from the fog, I take a step back and the creak on the hardwood floor has Gerrick's eyes snap to mine. There is pure rage, hatred in them.

My entire body shivers.

He is death.

I quickly turn on my heel and bolt out of the combat room.

Neeshah was right. I need to stay the hell away from him.

# Chapter Four

That night, I was tossing and turning in my bed. The images of what Gerrick did keeps replaying in my mind. I can't believe he just killed someone, and not just anyone, he was our classmate. What will the school tell his family?

Was it an accident?

I don't think so, the way his eyes glimmered with rage was undeniable.

"Are you awake?" Aylee whispers into the darkness of our room. I can hear soft snoring from Neeshah.

"Yeah."

"Did you want to talk about what happened?" she asks me.

"Not really." I hear the bedsheets move and my bed dips with her weight.

"Move over." She touches my shoulder and I obey. I let Aylee slide into my bed next to me.

"I'm sorry you had to see that." She sits up against my pillows and brings my head to her chest, stroking my hair in a comforting rhythm.

"The images won't leave my mind. Every time I close my eyes, I see his lifeless body just lying there. There wasn't anything anyone could have done to save him." I feel the wetness of a lone tear roll down my cheek.

"Is this how our next five months are going to be? Survive or die?" I shudder at the thought.

**You will not die, Special One.**

"Did you say something?" I turn and look up at Aylee, but she shakes her head in the dark.

That is weird. Where did that voice come from?

It sounded like a raspy old female's voice, like something only legends talk about.

I mentally shake it away.

I must be imagining it, I'm beyond exhausted.

"Try to get some sleep, I'm here, Ash." Aylee moves slightly and presses her lips against the top of my head. I knew having my best friend with me would give me comfort here at the Academy, but I never knew just how much.

"Love you," I say when the darkness finally takes hold of my body and mind.

* * *

*Knock...knock...* I roll over in bed and feel an empty spot where Aylee was last night. She must have gone back to her own bed once I'd fallen asleep.

"I'm not getting up," I manage to get out, half asleep.

"I will," Neesh pipes in, almost cheery. It's too damn early for that perkiness.

"What the fuck are you doing here?" she spits out.

I immediately sit up in bed and see Gerrick at the door.

What the fuck indeed.

"I need to see her!" He tries to push the door open, but Neesh is doing a good job at stopping it.

"Fat chance, I warned you yesterday. Leave her alone."

"I want to explain what happened; she needs to know," he begs.

"No."

"Ash, please let me in. I must talk to you." He ignores Neesh and tries to look around her. Once his eyes land on mine, I instantly get a flashback of his eyes from yesterday and his hands around Tyike's throat.

"Stay the fuck away from me," I say, barely a whisper.

"You heard her, fuck off, Gerrick."

"NO!" His anger is starting to boil over the edge.

"I'd be careful, water boy." Neesh's hands appear normal, but flames are starting to rise out of them.

I'm in complete shock, I didn't think she could wield such power yet.

Gerrick raises his hands in surrender. "Fine, I'm leaving." He starts walking backward away from our door but before he turns to leave, he smirks at me.

He knows he can always get to me, especially when Neesh and Aylee aren't around.

Fuck.

"That boy has some nerve." She shuts the door and leans her back against it.

"I give him some credit though, he's persistent," Aylee chimes in.

"You know he will find a way to get to me, he won't stop," I tell them, but I have a feeling they already knew that.

"We can see if you can switch classes to be with us?" Aylee adds in.

"I've already tried, no teacher wants to listen," Neesh tells us.

"You... you already tried? When?" I can't believe her.

"Ah... when Gerrick punched you unconscious. It was a no-brainer, that boy is trouble." Neeshah shows no remorse in her actions. I get where she is coming from, she is trying to look out for me but I'm not a child. I am a grown woman. A strong, independent Fae.

"Thanks for trying." I shrug, but I don't mean it.

Later that morning, my hand is ready to push open the combat training door when Mr. Rowenfield walks up next to me.

"There's no class today." He slams a piece of paper on the door that reads "Training cancelled until further notice." I groan, just my luck.

"What will I do now?" I ask him.

"Do extra studies... go to the library... find something useful to do." He turns on his heel and walks back from where he came.

The murmur of students is getting louder when they all start to read the piece of paper on the door.

"This is Gerrick's fault," Rikie says.

"He is a killer; he should be thrown out," Rakie agrees with her brother.

"He's still hot though," a girl next to me says while shrugging.

"Today's training should be interesting." *That* voice.

Everything around me just stops. It's like time has stood still. No one moves, no one utters a word. My breathing halts.

He's here... of course he is. Why hasn't anyone told him before us? Why isn't there an investigation happening?

"Training is cancelled, thanks to you," I bite out the

words, and I see all heads turn toward me. Shocked expressions mirror off each other.

"My fault? I'm not the one who died," Gerrick says as the students part a pathway for him to walk through.

"You are the one who *killed* him," I spit the words at him with such hate and rage in my voice.

My blood is starting to boil now. I can't even look at him without wanting to punch him in the throat, just to get him to stop talking.

"I did but, Fireball, it was a kill or be killed situation and I didn't want to die." He fucking smirks at me.

Who the fuck is this guy?

**Someone who you want to be on your side, Special One**

It's that voice again, is it my voice of reason?

Is that even such a thing?

I ignore that voice and take a step toward him.

"I challenge you." I can't believe I just said those words.

"You lose, you leave this academy."

"And if I win, Fireball?" He smirks at me, crosses his hands casually over his chest.

"It's your choice." Should I have said that? Probably not.

"A kiss."

"No fucking way! I rather be kicked out of the Academy than kiss you!" The audacity.

"Deal's a deal, Fireball." He uncrosses his arms and moves his left hand toward me, waiting for me to shake it.

"Do it," one kid says.

"You better win!" Rakie mutters.

"Why can't he kiss me?" the same girl whispers, but I'm pretty sure we all heard it.

I reach my right hand forward and shake his hand.

"Deal, but my choice of weapon." I smirk at him.

I am pretty good with a sword.

That is my biggest strength here, besides my water power, but it'll be moot when he is also a water wielder.

"Deal." He squeezes my hand in his.

"Tonight, when the moon is at its highest peak, in the courtyard." I drop his hand and turn on my heel.

What the fuck did I just do?

Aylee and Neeshah are going to murder me for this.

# Chapter Five

"You have got to be fucking kidding me, Aisling Midnight!!" She uses my full name, that's how I know I truly fucked up.

"I had to do something! I couldn't just let him kill more people. This way, if I win, he must leave."

"There! Right there, you said *if* I win! Ash, what were you thinking?" Her shoulders sag.

"I was trying to do the right thing." Neesh has been awfully quiet this entire conversation.

"I may not have known you my entire life, Ash, but this is incredibly stupid," Neesh finally adds her two cents in.

"It is, but it's done. I drew the challenge, and I must honor it." I get off my bed and walk toward the window in our room. I look up to the starry night and see the moon has reached the highest peak.

Below in the courtyard, it's completely empty. I wonder if Gerrick is lurking in the shadows, waiting for me.

"It's showtime." I pull my hair up into a tight bun on top of my head and nod to my two friends.

"You should wait here."

"No, we are coming with you." Aylee steps forward but I put my hand up to stop her.

"I'm not going to get killed, it's just a challenge. You know my skills with a sword, trust in that." I smile at her. Not sure if the smile reached my eyes, but I hope they both can respect my decision.

My feet crunch against the gravel on the pathway to the courtyard. There is no sound, only the sound of my breath and the pounding of my heart.

Why did I do this?

Was it to prove that I can fight him?

That I can challenge him, that I am worthy to be here.

Honestly, I have no fucking idea.

There is a large oak tree in the middle of the courtyard and no one to be seen. Strange, I declared the challenge in front of everyone, I naturally thought there would be some sort of crowd.

I don't see Gerrick anywhere.

The sword is heavy in my hands, not because of the weight of it, but the dread I'm about to use this against a student. I don't plan on killing him, just to win and get him to leave for good.

"You came," Gerrick steps out from the shadows. "I didn't think you would." His lips tilt up into a smirk.

"Of course, I would. It's my challenge, after all." I tilt my chin up to him, meeting his leveling gaze.

"Very well." He strides toward me and throws down his sword at his feet.

I take a step back, shocked at what he's just done. For a split second, I don't have the right words. Can it be that easy?

"Are you giving up?" I use his own tactics, and smirk at him. Two can play this game.

"If you really want me gone, then consider it done."

I take him in, he is still dressed in his fighting leathers, but he's got wet hair like he's just had a shower and run his fingers through it.

I wish I could run my fingers through it.

I mentally shake that thought away. There is no way I can find this man attractive. Not after everything he has done.

*He's killed someone,* I remind myself.

A nervous laugh bubbles up past my lips. "You're serious?" I ask him.

"I am." He takes a step back, tilting his head to watch my next move. It's like he's calculating me, wondering what I'm going to do next.

I wish I had that figured out, but I'm still lost. Confused.

My feet move and I'm closing the space between us.

"Pick up your sword!" I demand, poking him lightly in the chest with the tip of my sword.

"Are you sure you want to lose?" he taunts me. "I'm giving you an out here." He shrugs his shoulders, like he doesn't care whether he's here at the Academy or not.

"I want this to be a fair fight and I will win; I want you *gone.*" I poke him again but with a bit more force this time.

"I can't wait to kiss you, Fireball." He smirks while bending down to pick up the sword at his feet.

I take a step back, waiting.

He doesn't give me any time before he is swinging his sword toward me. I dodge it with a twist of my body, and I bring up my own sword to defend his second hit.

"You aren't bad." He chuckles.

I use my body weight to push his sword off mine.

"I had a good teacher," I snap out. I can't lose.

My teacher was my brother, he's somewhere on the front line and I'm determined to survive these next six months to go and find him.

I advance on my strike, getting the proper stance to bring my sword down on him, but he quickly dodges it. I recover and bring my sword back and plunge it toward his chest but the clatter of metal sounds in the empty courtyard.

He's good, I'll give him that.

***You need to shut him down, Special One***

That voice, where is it coming from? I quickly glance around the courtyard, but there is no one in sight besides Gerrick and me.

Gerrick takes advantage that I'm distracted and lands a death strike to the curve of my neck.

"If this was outside of those gates, Fireball. You'd be dead." He looks over to the entrance gates to the Academy. He isn't wrong. I was distracted and it could have cost me my life.

I tap his sword with mine, giving him the signal, he's won.

"Congratulations, Gerrick. You get to stay," I bluntly say.

"You could have had me there, what happened?" He sounds almost genuine... almost.

"Nothing." I sheathe my sword on my back.

"It's not nothing, Fireball. Something distracted you, but there isn't anyone here besides you and me." See, that doesn't make sense either.

"Why isn't there?" I fire back.

"I made sure it was just the two of us. Just in case you

did lose. I didn't want anyone to witness it." Oh.

"Thanks. Well, I better get back to my room." I turn on my heel.

"I won." He chuckles. "I will be claiming my kiss, Fireball." I freeze mid step.

Fuck, I forgot about that.

"Better get it over with," I bite out, not moving from my spot. If he wants it that bad, well, he can come and get it.

"It'll be on my terms, Ash." He walks right up to me, raises his hand in front of my face, and gently brushes his fingers against my cheek.

I internally shiver, the feeling of want and need start to rise to the surface.

*He's killed someone,* I keep reminding myself.

I'm seating next to a boy named Josh. He's been taking notes for me since I've missed a few of my Gaurdians classes, it's all about theory.

"Thanks." I lean over and look down at the desk in front of him.

He's drawing a griffin; we only learn about them in stories. It's legend that we have six Guardians who look after the realm of Inixiam. No one has ever reported seeing any, but if they had, the books and parchments are gone. There is no way to know for sure.

"It's no problem. I thought you'd be interested in this class." He shrugs and goes back to his drawing.

I listen intently to Mr. Tomb and he's now describing how there is a dragon in our realm who oversees the other five Guardians.

How is that even possible?

To think there is a boss who essentially oversees the other mythical creatures.

I wonder what it would be like to meet any one of them. The power they would radiate, the lifetime they would have witnessed. I am just in awe.

"Aisling, can you tell me what the Guardians are?" Mr. Tomb narrows in on me and I fidget in my seat. I have done plenty of studying back at home, but to be called upon in front of my peers is another thing.

"Ah. There is the griffin, the dragon of course, um, sea serpent, the phoenix, ouroboros. and..." I scratch the side of my arm, nervous to get this easy question wrong.

"Amarok," Josh whispers beside me.

"Yes, the amarok." I smile up at Mr. Tomb.

"If I wanted to ask you, Mr. Niles, I would have called upon you, but I think Miss Midnight can answer for herself. Don't you?" He arches an eyebrow at Josh.

"Yes, of course, sir." He bends his head to focus back to his drawing but instead he's just looking at it. Embarrassed? I would assume so.

"Thanks anyway," I whisper to him, but he doesn't acknowledge me.

"Can anyone tell me why we need the Guardians for the realm?" Mr. Tomb doesn't miss a beat in teaching his class. A student sitting two rows in front of me raises their hand.

"To keep the balance of magic, that is if the Guardians are real. Otherwise, it'll be evil outweighing good." She beams. Her blond hair perky at the base of her neck, tight strong shoulders, and she's dressed in a black dress. I didn't think we were allowed to wear anything else but our fighting leathers.

Unless that's just me since I've only attended combat

training so far.

"That is correct, it is a myth, but it keeps everyone in check... except for the Nurrigorgen. They think all magic belongs to them, and that is why we are at war with them. We are trying to restore the balance to the realm and magic itself." He nods at her.

"Shouldn't the Lords be the ones to protect us?" Rakie asks. She does have a point.

"They do, they are the ones who created and built this academy, who help keep balance in each court and drive those nasty humans away... but enough questions. That'll be it for class today. Make sure you write a piece on which Guardian you'd prefer to protect you and why." He walks away from the front of the class to his desk at the far end of the room.

Which one would I choose?

"I'd pick the sea serpent." Josh chimes in.

"Why's that?" I follow him out of class and down a narrow hallway to the main building where meals are served. I am starving.

"I think controlling the sea would be amazing!" He beams.

If only he knew, water isn't all that it's cracked up to be... I should know.

"What court are you from?" I'm usually a good guesser with people, but Josh stumps me. Could he possibly be a child of a mixed court?

"Air." He nods, "What are you?" he asks.

Shouldn't it be obvious?

"Water." I shrug, the conversation would have gotten better but he just quickly walks away from me.

"Is it something I said?" I call after him.

Weird.

# Chapter Six

I never thought of my magic in depth before. It's not something one really thinks about. You are born in whatever court you live in, in Archurillia, our homeland, and that's the element you have for life. A baby born in Fire Court will present fire powers, Air Court will have air powers etc... I have heard of legends where a Fae was born in their particular court but presented with all five elemental powers, but that's like the Mythical Guardians all over again.

You never hear about it; there's no village talk of it, and there isn't any documentation to claim it either, yet we are learning about it at the Academy. That makes me question everything.

Is whatever we learn here kept to secrecy? Surely not. It can't be that simple, someone would have spilled the beans over the years.

There is also a rumour circling that every five decades or so—or if something tragically happens—then one of the Fae Lords who are unmarried must find someone to marry. The Lord may choose anyone, but it's more preferred someone from the Academy. Their strength and ability to defend themselves are good indications to rule a court.

Unfortunately, whoever is chosen doesn't get a choice in the matter.

We must stand by the law.

It's not impossible for a Lord to marry someone outside of their ruling court, although it's never been done before.

Once chosen, you must marry the Lord and become the Lady of that court. I have done some research before coming to the Academy and there is only one Lord who isn't married. The Lord of Fire is without a wife.

I close the book I'm supposed to be reading and zone out of the library's windows.

They have large bay windows that overlook the sea and beyond to the east is the island of Vardirian. I've heard stories of how stunning Spring Court is and to the west of us is Primthod. Night Court is supposed to be magical. Southeast of us is the island of Edox and that is the island of the humans and their forbidden creatures.

That's the island where our war began.

Where our war continues to be.

"Daydreaming?" Josh places a stack of books next to where I'm sitting, pulls the chair out, spins it, and sits down with the back of the chair to his front. He rests his forearms along the top, effortlessly.

"Something like that." I never break eye contact from the ocean and its waves rippling through the water.

It's calming and has a certain pull to be near it.

I wonder if there's a way I could ask a teacher's permission to go beyond the wards, just to sink my toes into the sand, plunge my hands into the water to get the radiating energy from it.

"Have you decided which Guardian you'll choose to do your paper on?" he asks me, admiring the view himself.

"I haven't decided yet, it's hard to choose if you know nothing about them. I've spent the last hour in here trying to find any kind of information on them, but I just can't." Feeling defeated, I sag more in my seat.

"I know we were all taught about the myth, the legend of them, but nothing prepared me for this...What about you?" I look to the left of me and study him, really look at him. He's cute, with his curly brown hair framing his neck and forehead. The point of his ears is just visible, his pale blue eyes, and the slightest green shine. Hmm, maybe his parents are from two different courts.

"I was thinking the the griffin, I like the look of it but I do like the sea serpent." That would make sense since he was drawing it in class and he did mention the other one as well.

"You should focus on what draws to you." He isn't wrong.

"Thanks, you should do the same." I pick up my notebook and leave Josh to his studies.

"See you." I turn my back to him and walk out of the library.

What he said does make sense, I should focus on what draws to me, but I honestly have no idea. Maybe I should write a pro and con list? But I don't know anything about them.

I silently groan.

My feet take me to the courtyard, and I sit on the wooden bench that surrounds the oak tree, thinking about my family back home. I sure do miss them, but I know I'm better off than staying there.

My dad is looking after my oldest sister, Emmie, who

was injured in an attack against her and my mother. That attack took my mother's life.

*"Girls!! Girls!!" my father yells out from downstairs.*

*I groggily open my eyes and pull a robe over the top of my nightgown. Opening my bedroom door, I look down the corridor and my other sisters have done the same.*

*"What is going on?" Violet asks.*

*"I don't know but it sounds urgent," Kourt answers her once she steps out from her bedroom.*

*"Let's go downstairs and find out," I tell them.*

*We follow each other down the stairs and see Father in a panic.*

*"What's happened?" I rush to his side.*

*"There's...." He starts to sob. "...been an attack." He finally gets the words out around inhaling deep breaths, trying to compose himself.*

*"What do you mean?" Terreasa asks him.*

*"Your sister, Emmie, and Mother never came home, so I sent word to look for them. I've just been told there's been an attack and it's not good... oh, girls." He opens his arms out and we all rush in to give him and ourselves comfort.*

*"Do you know anything else?" I quietly ask him.*

*"No, we are waiting for more answers..." He trails off.*

*"I should have sent word sooner, maybe this could all have been avoided."*

*"Oh, Father, you weren't to know. We know Emmie and Mother usually have late nights when the evening markets are running," Kourt tries to reassure father.*

*A few moments later, there's a knock on our front door.*

*"I'll go get it." I start to leave Father's embrace.*

*"No. You all stay here; I'll go see who it is." Father removes himself from our arms and slowly walks toward the front door.*

*I think everyone in this room is holding their breath.*

*Could it be that bad?*

*An attack? Maybe they were just mugged and were a little hurt and taken to the court infirmary.*

*I strain my ears to hear what is being said but I can't make any words out.*

*"Can you..." I ask the others but they shake their heads. They must hear exactly what I do.*

*"I'm so sorry..." one of the strangers says.*

*NOO!" My father howls the words, and his sobs are so loud, they vibrate through all of us together.*

*Silence falls between us girls.*

*Something terrible has happened.*

*My father's heavy footsteps make it to the living room, we all turn to his direction, and he only says, "Mother is dead."*

*"Emmie?" I ask.*

*"Badly hurt... they don't know if she'll make it through the night."*

*Those words will haunt me for the rest of my life.*

It's never been the same since that night. I know my father has the resources to care for Emmie, she didn't make a full recovery from the attack. My father used to be the right-hand man to Lord Marcus of Water Court. Until the attack, Dad would have been hardly home and that's when my sister, Kourt, who's the second eldest daughter decided to remain home and marry instead of attending the Academy. Then you have my two younger sisters, Violet and Terreasa, who are twins. I'm not sure what their intentions are, but I couldn't sit around and wait for the war to reach our front doorsteps. I decided to take my life into my own hands, and that's why I'm here. I don't want to be, that's been clear from my first day, but as the weeks go by, it's getting easier.

To think we only have five months left.

"Is this seat taken?" That familiar voice floats around the courtyard and it brings back that night of our sword fight and how I lost.

I still owe him a kiss. How could I forget about that?

"Yes," I answer but I don't look up at him. I feel him, it vibrates through my entire body.

"I'll stand."

"What do you want, Gerrick?" I don't have the energy to deal with his shit today.

"I just wanted to see how you are doing, and if you were doing anything later?" What in the world?

"I'm busy, and if I was free, I wouldn't waste my time on *you!*" I stand up from the bench and start walking away from him.

"You'll give in to me one of these days, Fireball."

"You just don't know when to stay away, do you?" Neeshah steps out from behind the brick wall. How long has she been standing there? Is Aylee with her?

"I have my own free will, so does Fireball." He just smirks at her, like she's not a threat, but she has one hell of a temper.

"Sure, there's *that*, but I told you to stay... away!" She steps closer to Gerrick, but he still isn't fazed by her.

"What are you going to do? Report me? Run to the teacher like a scared little bumblebee?" He pretends to shiver in his boots.

"Don't mock me, asshole!" she yells, her hands suddenly become flames.

"You can't use magic on another student without a

teacher present, Neesh!" I tell her with a firm but friendly tone. I don't want that anger pointed at me, no thank you.

"Give it your best shot," Gerrick taunts.

Within seconds, Neeshah is aiming balls of fire toward Gerrick, but he puts up a water shield every time she shoots a flame from her hands.

"STOP IT!" I scream, the ground beneath us moves, but I don't pay it a second thought when Neeshah starts growing larger flames from her hands and forms them into arrows. They glide faster in the air and with her aim, I doubt she'll miss.

"STOP!" I scream again, I can't let this happen.

Gerrick isn't fast enough for the arrows, he's got two fire marks on his chest and his right shoulder, but he doesn't falter, he just tries to keep up with blocking her.

"ENOUGH!!" I scream louder. I can feel the tingling sensation I get when I use my water power. This must end. I need it to. I don't want anyone to get seriously hurt. Not on my behalf.

Neeshah forms a large fire arrow. I'm scared that if she makes her target then it'll be the end of Gerrick. How can I live with that?

"I... SAID... ENOUGH!!" I raise my palms in the air and aim it at Neeshah. "Please forgive me," I whisper and water sprays from my palms and wets Neesh from behind. She's distracted long enough that she turns around and faces me. I watch as Gerrick retreats in the opposite direction, but he stops for a split second and blows me a kiss.

Is he fucking serious right now?

"Why would you do that?" Neesh looks pained, like I just killed something inside of her.

"You were going to *kill him*. How can you just stand there and think that is okay?"

"He has to be stopped and if I am the one to do it, then so be it." She shrugs.

I don't know who I'm more scared of, Gerrick or her.

"Neesh, why are you wet? And why are you so angry?" Aylee appears out of nowhere and walks to stand in the middle of us, looking at both of us with confusion on her face.

"It doesn't matter, it's over." I emphasize the word 'over' because it is. I can't share a room with someone who thinks killing is okay. I can't have a friend who is willing to let someone die because they find them annoying. Yes, Gerrick did kill someone as well, but was it more a kill or be killed situation?

Plus, I think he can be redeemed.

Honestly, do I even believe that?

"I'm too tired to get into this again. I'm sure Neesh can do the explaining here. I have elements class in an hour. I want to try and reserve my strength for that.

# Chapter Seven

Elements class is interesting to say the least. Mrs. Storm has unique powers. She's from Air Court, so she can control the sky, but she only can control storms. I thought we could control all aspects of our element, but she proved us wrong today.

I look around the room, but I don't see Gerrick anywhere and we share every class together. Maybe after the attack from Neeshah, he decided to stay away from me after all.

"Who are you looking for?" Josh leans in from his seat to whisper into my ear.

"No one." The heat rises from my neck to my cheeks. I know I shouldn't be looking for him, but I've gotten so used to him.

"I'm sure, it doesn't look like no one." He raises an eyebrow.

"It is, someone who doesn't deserve my time."

"Do I deserve your time?" He winks at me.

He fucking winks.

Is this boy trying to flirt with me?

"Of course, but not like that, Josh, you're my friend."

"Yeesh, friend zoned." He laughs. "Don't worry, you're not my type anyway." With that, he leans back away from me and sits up straighter in the chair. Zoning me out, he focuses on the teacher and whatever she's been trying to tell us.

I laugh.

I know I just friend zoned him, but to have it done back to me so casually, I don't think that's happened to me before.

"Well, I hope someone here is your type, Josh. You deserve that happiness." I pat his shoulder.

"Oh, there is..." He trials off, but before I can ask him further about it, Mrs. Storm has her last speech for the day.

"Class, I want you all to focus on the source of your powers. I want you to channel what you're feeling each time and harness it. Use it to your advantage. Heaven forbid, you freeze up in the middle of a battle. Get used to the pressure, the sensation, and use it. Next class, I will be testing each and every one of you. So, practice!" I gather my books and leave class. I have this urge to go see Gerrick, to see if he's okay. I know Aylee and Neesh will be so pissed off at me, but I feel like taking the risk. Can I try to sneak into the boys' dorms? I know he did for me. Even though I found that completely annoying, but do I owe him one?

Fuck it!

My feet change direction and I walk down the dark corridor, past the combat room and down a flight of stairs to the courtyard. That very courtyard to hold a few memories between Gerrick and me. I enter the very large building with the door slightly ajar. I slip past it and hope no one saw me. It's not like it's forbidden to enter the opposite sex's wing, but it is frowned upon.

Standing in the middle of the corridor to the boys' dorm. I have come to the realization I have no idea which room belongs to Gerrick.

Shit.

"Can I help you?" A nervous boy comes to a halt in front of me.

"Girls aren't allowed in the boys' dorms."

"I know, I just wanted to drop off some notes from elemental class, can you help me?" I really hope this shy student will help me and not go running to the teachers to turn me in.

"Oh... ah." He nervously switches his stance.

"If it's too much to ask, I can try and find someone else to ask." I don't want him to feel guilty for telling me. I know the type, they'll beat themselves up for giving me the information and not telling on me, but if he does give me the information then he will beat himself up about it. I think it would be best if I didn't have him help me.

"He's right down the hall. Last door to your right, you can't miss it." He quickly hurries off. I didn't think he had it in him, woo!

I silently cheer for him.

My feet carry me along the hallway to Gerrick's room, I pass maybe twenty rooms on either side and make it to his. Standing in front of the door, I'm starting to have second thoughts. This is a bad idea.

Really bad idea.

It's now or never.

I raise my fist to the door and knock twice.

"I don't want to see anyone today, fuck off!" Gerrick yells from his side of the door.

"I refuse to leave." I hold my breath for five seconds, and if he doesn't open the door in that time, then I'll just leave.

I hear loud commotion coming from behind the door and when I'm about to press my ear against it, the door opens.

Gerrick is standing there in his leather pants and he's shirtless.

His shoulders bulge with muscles, the dark swirls of his tattoo cover most of the right side of his chest and his abs... they are so defined, so tight. I wonder what they would feel like, are they as hard as they look?

Good heavens.

I'm in trouble.

"Fireball." He puts one hand on top of the doorframe and leans in a little closer to me.

"I came to see how you were doing, you haven't been to class today."

"Checking up on me, that's cute." He smirks.

The bastard.

"I shouldn't have come." I go to turn around, but he grabs me by the wrist.

"I'm sorry, please come in before anyone sees you." He steps inside but pulls me along with him. I stand in his room and take it in.

It's set up like our dorms, but he isn't rooming with anyone. How is that possible?

"Get special treatment?" I say, tilting my chin to his room.

"Something like that." He lets go of my wrist and takes a seat on his bed.

"Can you put on a shirt or something?"

"Why? Am I too distracting for you, Fireball?" he teases.

"As a matter of fact, yes." Who knew I could be this honest with him.

"Fine." He gets off the bed and walks over to his wardrobe and puts on a white shirt.

"Look, I wanted to talk to you, but it's been extremely hard with your friends around." He motions with his hand for me to sit in the chair opposite his bed. I take it.

"I know, they are very protective, but I am my own person. I can make up my own mind, and if I do things that are bad then I must live with those regrets or consequences for those actions." It's all true though, they can try to protect me from anything bad, and I would do the same, but I am a grown woman. I have to live and learn."

"Wise words," he utters.

"So, what did you want to talk to me about?" I cross my right ankle over the other, waiting to see what he has to say.

"The first combat match, you and me. I didn't mean for you to blackout, I don't even know why I did it. I guess I didn't want to lose, and you seemed like an easy target, but you weren't so, my rage took over. I'm sorry." He brushes his hand through his already messy hair.

"It happens and I've learned from that. I haven't lost a combat match since." Also true, he's made me a better fighter. I wanted to prove I'm not some weak person who will die the minute I step on the battlefield.

"The second combat match... where I killed someone. That... that was also my rage and he utter words just before he died and all I saw was red."

"What did he say?"

"I will never repeat those words, Fireball." Now I am even more curious.

"Did he have to die because he uttered those words?"

"Yes, and I don't regret it. I'd probably do it all over again but there would be something I'd change."

"What?"

"You wouldn't be watching... seeing your face the minute it happened made me sick to my stomach. The pure disgust on your face made me feel things, things I never thought I could feel." He leans over and takes my hand in his.

"You, Ash, you make me feel so many emotions. Good and the bad. I have no idea what to do with them." He rubs his thumb over the back of my hand in circular motions. It's comfortable but I don't know how to take what he's saying.

Does he have feelings for me?

Do I have feelings for him?

"This is too much." I pull my hand out of his and I quickly leave his room.

I can't do this right now.

I just can't.

# Chapter Eight

I need to let off steam, my entire being is going haywire. I need to get myself back into control.

I never asked permission from a teacher to leave the grounds to go to the beach, but that is where I'm headed.

Rules be damned.

My boots crunch under the sand and I find a nearby rock to take them off.

My feet touch the softness of the sand, it's squishing between my toes. I can taste the saltiness of the sea in the air. The freshness of being outside of the wards is rushing into my nose and the wind singing songs of love and pure happiness dances around my entire being.

This, this is where I belong.

My feet take the last steps toward the water and immediately I'm greeted with the cold and wetness of the waves.

This. Is. Heaven.

I focus everything on my magic, where it comes from and how it makes me feel. Once I feel the tingles swirling around my nerves, I know I can start to control it.

I twist my hand and wiggle my fingers slowly and the water before me starts to turn into a swirl, higher and higher it gets from the sand. It's beautiful. I've only been able to create bubbles or small animals from memory, but nothing like this. Nothing this large and it makes me wonder what else I can do.

I close my eyes and feel the magic radiating from me. I inhale a deep breath and raise both of my hands and flick them out to both of my sides. I hear a whoosh and I open my eyes to see the ocean is parted right down the middle. In front of me is clear sand and a two-meter water wall.

It's amazing.

I did that.

I hold my hands in that position, waiting to see how long I can hold it, but before long the wall starts to collapse and turn into a flat surface in a matter of seconds.

The stronger I get, I bet I can hold it for longer.

The library is a good start to research of what other Water Fae can do with their powers.

I look left and right of me at the shoreline, not a soul insight, but I don't risk it any longer. I am outside of the wards. I don't want to get into trouble, or worse, get caught by the Nurrigorgen.


"What are you doing outside of the wards?" Gerrick surprises me at the side gate to the Academy. It's the only gate that's not guarded and I don't see why it should be, it's under a bricked archway covered by large bushes and trees, which is where I'm standing now. If you don't know what to look for, no one would know it was there.

"None of your business," I say, walking past him. He

grabs my wrist, halting me in my tracks. I turn around to face him.

"It's dangerous out there, especially if you don't know what to look out for." He sounds sincere, but I'm not buying it.

"I can take care of myself, Gerrick." I try to yank my wrist free, but he only holds it tighter.

"Take it from me, I know what those *things* can do to us." His face turns up in disgust.

"So, the rumors are true then, you've seen them… fought them?" I can't help my curiosity.

"I have, and it's…" He pauses to try and find the right words. "Horrifying."

"Good to know." I try to pull my wrist free again, but this time he lets it go. I just stand here, staring at him, not knowing why he's even out here.

"Sneaking out?" I raise my eyebrow at him.

"I needed some air." He turns away from me and looks toward the floor, not meeting my eyes.

"I know that feeling," I say, almost as a whisper but he heard it.

He looks up at me and his eyes turn dark. He takes a step toward me, and I move a step away from him. My back immediately hits the archway wall. I'm trapped.

"I've wanted to do this the moment I saw you, Fireball." He closes the distance between us and reaches his hand up to my cheek and runs his thumb over my lips.

I look into his eyes and all I see is pure desire. I lick my lips and he takes that as an invitation.

He closes the remaining distance and grabs my face with his other hand, and our lips touch for the first time. It's soft and warm.

It's taken me by surprise, but it soon turns into something heated. I grab his shirt at the collar and bring him in closer. Our tongues dance to a new rhythm, slow at first but Gerrick moves both hands down my shoulders, my arms, my hips, and finally they find their destination. My ass.

He picks me up by my ass and presses me back against the wall.

I feel every hard inch of his body on mine. It's sending me crazy.

Lost in the sensation, I barely hear the cough from the right of us.

Gerrick parts from us to see who it is, and he freezes.

"What?" I whisper.

He drops me, my feet connect to the ground, and I'm pissed off. How dare he drop me like that?

I'm shielded by his shoulder so I can't see who it is but from Gerrick's posture, he knows exactly who it is.

"Gerrick." The voice almost sounds like a growl. It's so deep and smooth, almost like honey.

"Uncle." What? That can't be right. I peek around his arm and when I see the man standing there, we lock eyes and something shifts inside of me. It's almost like this electricity has been pulling at my entire being for my whole life, but in this exact moment it's snapped back into place, where it belongs. It's like where it should be, and then all of a sudden, the feeling is gone.

The man turns his heated gaze to his nephew, it's almost like pure hatred.

"I...ah...mean, General." Gerrick shifts his feet, he's really uncomfortable. I take it he understands the look in his eyes too, but I don't get it. I'm so confused by everything that's just happened.

"There's going to be an announcement, head to the courtyard immediately," the general says, but I don't wait a second. I move past Gerrick and don't waste any time by looking back. I hurry off and leave Gerrick with his uncle.

In the courtyard, I find Aylee and Neeshah. I stand next to them, trying to remain calm and put on a face to conceal what just happened.

"Where have you been?" Neeshah whispers.

"I needed a minute to myself," I whisper back, not giving her anything. I can't, not until I figure things out myself.

Moments later, Mr. Rowenfield takes the stage that was built for this occasion, and he starts talking about how there's only three months left, and we need to step up our training.

The general walks across the stage and stands next to Mr. Rowenfield, his eyes scan the crowed of students and then our eyes lock again, it feels like an eternity when Aylee nudges my arm and breaks our contact.

What is that?

Why do I get instant zaps of energy coursing through my body?

"Do you know him?" Aylee asks.

My cheeks heat, I want to tell her what just happened between Gerrick and me, and then when his uncle... the general caught us, but I'm still trying to wrap my head around it myself.

"No, I don't," I rasp out. That's not exactly a lie.

"It doesn't look that way."

"This is General Dorian from Fire Court; he is the most skilful warrior Archurillia has to offer. Please pay attention to what he has to say, students." Mr. Rowenfield leaves the stage.

A general? But he doesn't look that much older than me. I wonder how he got his title.

I listen to every word he has to say.

He will be staying to watch us train in combat and offer any advice he can while he's here for the week.

I have no words, other than fuck.

# Chapter Nine

"**A**re you sure you don't know him?" Aylee is grilling me again in our dorm room.

"Yes, I've told you everything… I don't know him." I told her everything that happened between me and Gerrick. I told her without Neeshah being present. I don't need her hothead to know… especially with her feelings toward Gerrick, she would prefer him to be dead. Not something that's going to happen, since he has two war generals in his family, that's insane.

"Good morning, students, I'll be here to watch and assess you sparring today." General Dorian walks in a line in front of us.

"Will this count to our final grade?" one student, I don't remember her name, calls out.

"No, this is my personal assessment." He stops and stares right at Gerrick. I wonder if he's sending a silent message to be on his best behavior or to show everyone what he's made of... and we all know too well what his full potential is.

He has the entire Academy here; I wonder if this is what it'll be like on assessment day. Everyone looking around at each other, not knowing if any of us will make it. If we manage to pass, will be stay alive on the front lines of the war? What would happen if we failed? I've never heard of anyone staying back and repeating another six months.

"Good luck." Aylee squeezes my shoulder; I know her and Neeshah will have no problem with combat hand-to-hand. I've been training every spare hour I can get between classes, and they've helped but I won't know if I've improved until I am on that mat.

"You too." I smile at her. Not that she needs it.

"The aim for today isn't to kill. You save that for war. I am here to assess the way you handle yourself in combat, the way you work out what's in front of you and your quick thinking. Those are the main things that will keep you alive." He looks down at a clipboard and starts calling out names who've been paired together.

"Aylee and Taylor take the mat."

"You've got this," I call after her.

"Neeshah and Josh." I give her the thumbs-up. I hope I don't get called, I want to watch them both and cheer them on.

"Aisling and Gerrick." Fuck!

Did he do that on purpose? I can't be paired with Gerrick for so many reasons.

I walk to the right of the room to the only empty mat. He's called out half of the students and they've begun sparring.

"We meet here again, Fireball." He smirks at me when my feet touch the mat.

"Care to take it easy on me this time?" I ask nicely.

"Not a chance." There's a glint in his eyes.

"At least *try* not to kill me." I tilt my head in a challenge.

Just like before, he lifts his right hand and motions his pointy finger to come to him. I'm more nervous than scared this time around. I know what to expect of Gerrick as a fighter. He is strong and quick, but I've learned to be quicker.

"Come on, Fireball, show me what you've got." Gerrick motions his hand again and I freeze.

### You need to win this, Special One

It's that voice. I quickly glance around the room, and I don't see where it would come from.

"Aisling?" Gerrick takes a step toward me. If he's using my full name, then he must be concerned.

"I'm okay, let's do this." I mentally shake the voice away and focus on the task ahead.

I take a step toward him, and just like he did, I motioned with my right hand for him to come get me. He takes another step toward me and nods.

"Let's do this, Fireball." He lunges for me, trying to throw a punch to my face but I quickly dodge him. I land a blow to the right side, just below his ribs. He grunts.

I gather my bearings and stand up straight, ready for another attack. Gerrick races forward, he successfully lands a punch to my stomach.

I groan in instant pain; the wind being knocked out of me is unpleasant but barrable.

Wincing, I stand and turn to face him, I can't have my back to him too long or the fight will be over.

This time, I go for the attack. I charge toward him and throw my fist back with as much force as I can muster, and I connect with his face. His hands immediately fly to his cheekbone. He raises his eyebrows in confusion, or is he impressed? I can't tell.

I don't take long to land another blow to his stomach, I'm greeted with rock-hard abs, but I don't dwell on that. I quickly crouch down and kick his legs from under him.

He had no chance to figure out my moves. I was quick.

I launch onto him, landing another punch to his face, this time right square to his right eye.

"Do you yield?" I call.

"No," he barely gets out.

"Yield!" I yell at him. I don't want to keep punching him, but I land one to his chest.

My legs have straddled either side of his hips.

"I like you here." He's recovered and smirks up at me.

"You've got to be fucking joking!" I clench my jaw.

I go to get off him, but he holds me in place.

"Can we do this later?" He winks at me.

I punch him so hard in the jaw he almost looks surprised.

I roll off him and land on the mat beside him.

"Get up!" I yell down at him.

"No."

"Yield!" I yell again.

I am so fucking frustrated; he's making this into a mockery now.

"You want me to actually fight you?" he asks, all serious now.

"Yes! That's the fucking point here." I place my hands on my hips, annoyed that he even has to ask this.

"What seems to be the problem here?" General Dorian approaches us, I instantly feel tingles up and down my spine.

Attraction? He is devastatingly handsome. His amber

eyes narrow on Gerrick. Did I just see a hint of purple? I look again and it's gone, did I imagine that? His dark brown curls frame his face and reach the back of his neck but short enough it's not touching the top of his fighting leathers. I wonder what it would feel like to lace my fingers through it.

His black fighting leathers just do no justice. They leaves nothing to the imagination.

"Nothing," I manage to say.

He nods and walks away. Leaving me heated in the cheeks and Gerrick staring.

"What?"

"Nothing."

"How are you related to the fire general?" He stands and faces me; we are merely two feet apart.

"My mother... his sister, she fell in love with my father from Water Court." There is sadness in his voice.

"She died after she gave birth to me."

"I am so sorry." I too know what it is like to lose a mother, but I don't tell him that. Now isn't the place to talk about our mothers.

"Can we please finish this?" I ask too nicely.

He doesn't hesitate, he grabs me by the wrist and flings me to the mat. He does it without any effort.

My back slams onto the mat with a thud.

He braces himself to throw a punch to my face, but I quickly dodge it. I buck my back off the mat and kick Gerrick in the face with my boot. It knocks him backward and I kick myself up off the mat and launch at him. I land another punch to his face, again and again.

He tries to block each blow, but I'm too quick.

"Yield?" I ask him.

"No!" he yells.

I land a punch to his gut and quickly stand. My boot is

pressed against his throat. I can squish his windpipe, blocking off all oxygen to his brain.

"Do you yield?" I yell down at him.

"Yes." He manages to tap the mat.

I let out a long breath.

I did it.

The entire gym erupts into cheers.

I didn't realize everyone had stopped sparring to watch us fight it out. Gerrick is the most feared combat warrior here, and I just bested him.

I remove my foot from Gerrick's throat and offer my hand. He takes it without a word.

"YAY!" Aylee rushes toward me and wraps me in her arms.

"Well done." Neesh nods approval.

"Thanks guys." I smile at them.

The crowed dwindles and Gerrick approaches me. He looks nervous, he is grabbing the back of his neck. He meets my eyes and starts moving his mouth, but no words seem to escape.

"What is it?"

"I... ah... wanted to see if you..." He doesn't finish his sentence when General Dorian walks toward us and stands right next to him.

He crosses his arms over his chest, somehow, he always looks pissed off at Gerrick.

"Gerrick, a word." He doesn't look my way, his heated gaze zeroes on his nephew.

Gerrick and General Dorian walk off out of the gym and toward the main entrance where the teacher's offices are.

Does he blame him for his sister's death? Is that why he is always cold toward him? Every time they are together there isn't much spoken between them. It's just awkward silence. Has it always been like that with them? I can't imagine how he is with Gerrick's dad.

I would think it would be difficult, especially both being generals. I wonder if they cross paths being both leaders, but they are from two different courts.

Maybe I can ask Gerrick later, although I don't want to pry into his family too much.

I sure wouldn't want him digging into my family history.

There would be a lot to uncover, and an unsolved murder as well. Not something you bring up in an average conversation.

# Chapter Ten

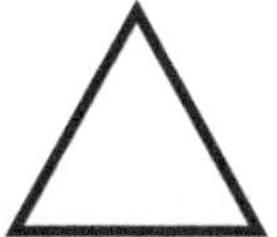

I've done some research into water element at the library.

There are some rare powers that only certain Fae can wield. That gives me motivation to see where the limit is to my powers.

"Are you going to practice your control?" Josh asks me in elemental class.

"No, I think I'm going to push my limits today." I've been practicing my control at the beach every day this past week, and I've been getting pretty good. He doesn't need to know about that though. I rather keep that information to myself.

"How are you going with your control?"

"It's coming along, I keep sending off mini earth rumbles when

Aylee and..." His eyes widen.

"I'm sorry... what?" I mimic his shocked face. Aylee and Josh?

How come I didn't know about this?

Was Aylee the type he was referring to the other week?

Why hasn't she told me herself?

She knows about what happened with Gerrick!

"Don't stop on my account." I plaster on a smile.

I silently groan, why can't I share the same classes as Aylee? I would have liked to ask her this myself. Instead, I'll get the information from Josh.

Why hasn't she told me back in our dorm room?

"I... ah..." He grabs the back of his neck, clearly embarrassed.

"We've been sort of seeing each other."

"How long?"

"A couple of weeks, I saw her studying in the library and I have never seen a more beautiful woman in my life." The way he gushes about her, could this be fated mates?

I've only read about it and heard stories passed down from generations, but I've never seen it firsthand.

I'm about to ask him about it when Mrs. Storm enters the room.

"Class, we will break up into two groups. Offense and defense," Mrs. Storm says. There goes our conversation. I will have to ask Aylee when we break for lunch.

"Will we be using our powers on each other?" a student in the back of the class calls out.

"Don't be ridiculous, Michael."

"Then how can we use our power defensively?" Michael asks her.

"You'll be taking turns using a dummy and myself. I know how to deflect any power." This class has just gotten more interesting.

"All right, this half will be offense." She points to the left of the room "And this will be defense." She points to the right of the room.

"Once we've gone through every student, you will swap roles. Got it?" The class say yes in unison.

"How would that even work? Shouldn't the dummy be for defense as it can't use power and Mrs. Storm to be offense?" I whisper to Josh. He just nods his head in agreement.

"The dummy is charmed to send out the smallest of power that won't harm any of you, if you have a question for me, Aisling. Ask it, don't whisper to another student of mine." Shit. I've been called out; I can feel my cheeks heat from the embarrassment.

Josh bumps his shoulder against mine, giving me comfort.

I'm standing behind Josh in our offense line and I'm fourth from the front. I'm just glad I'm not going first; I don't want to freeze up on the spot. Especially after the little embarrassing stunt.

I watch in awe when a fire student's hands completely light into a flame and he moves his right hand to behind him and slings a fireball at Mrs. Storm. Within a split second, she puts up a weather cloud to deflect the fire.

"Well done, Asher."

He walks to the back of the line and the next student steps forward.

I believe it's an earth wielder, I've never seen anyone actually try to wield the earth.

"You got this, Mike!" Asher calls out from behind the line.

Mike takes a stance in front of Mrs. Storm and his entire body relaxes. I wish I was at the front so I could see what he's doing but everything is eerily quiet in here.

"Mike, I need you to concentrate." Mrs. Storm tells him. Is he not wielding any magic? Can he?

"Do you feel that?" Josh whispers from in front of me, and as soon as he says it, I feel it. My feet begin to shake, the glass starts to wobble on the desk in the far corner.

"He's doing it!" Asher calls out.

I'm stunned.

I've never seen anything like it.

A large rock forms right in front of Mike, blocking his path to Mrs. Storm.

"Well done, Mike, but you were supposed to be on offense, not defense. Let's get rid of the rock, and try again." Mrs. Storm patience seems to be dwindling.

It doesn't take a second for the last word to leave her lips when small fragments of the rock start flying toward her.

She blocks each and every one with her cloud shield.

"That's my boy!" Asher cheers his friend on.

"That is amazing," I whisper to Josh.

"Most impressive, Mike, you can go back into line." The smile on the teacher's face is evident. She is impressed.

"My turn," Josh says more to himself than to me.

"You've got this," I say encouraging him.

I've never seen his power up and close before. I know he's from Air Court so this should be an interesting match with Mrs. Storm.

"Let's see what you've got, Josh."

He takes a step forward and a bubble forms around him and the teacher. I've only read about that power in books at the library. I wanted to research all types of magic, as I want to know what type of water magic to use.

Once the bubble is secured, you can't hear anything, you can't see anything. It's like he's blocked off the entire class from seeing inside. Why would he do that?

Is he going to murder Mrs. Storm and doesn't want us to see it?

I mentally shake that thought, that is just being stupid.

Within moments, the bubble is down, and Mrs. Storm is gasping for air.

What the fuck just happened?

"Well... done," She coughs twice. "Josh, that was most... impressive."

She takes a seat at her desk to gather herself. Every student in her class is wide-eyed and gaping mouths.

"What did you do?" I ask Josh.

"I formed a protective bubble, blocking outside from viewing in, and I withdrew the air from within." Holy shit.

I've never seen or read anything like that.

"You're up, Aisling." Mrs. Storm has composed herself and is now standing in front of our line.

Shit.

"You sure you don't want to rest?" I ask her, trying to worm my way out of this. I've used my power before, lots of times, but that was just me and the ocean. I've never done it in front of a crowd before.

Josh turns around, stops to the side of me, and squeezes my shoulder.

"You can do this." He offers me a sweet smile. I wish I had that sort of confidence in me. I watch as he walks to the back of the line. I take that step forward and clench my fists.

This is the time where I wanted to show what my power can do, but will I take that risk? Probably not.

"I'm not ready."

"Yes, you are, let's go, Aisling. I don't have all day." She is growing impatient with me.

I inhale a deep breath and close my eyes. I can feel the energy flowing in my veins and the tingling sensation every time I use my magic.

I visualize what I want my magic to do, and I open my

palms up, facing them at Mrs. Storm and let the flow of magic leave my body, along with the icy particles directed at the teacher.

"You can do better than that." Mrs. Storm almost laughs.

I open my eyes and it's like I'm seeing her for the first time.

She's tall, brown wavy hair, freckles on her entire face. Her lips pursed in frustration or boredom and narrowed pale blue eyes.

She is wearing tight black leather pants and black boots, but instead of wearing fighting leathers all over she has a pale blue tunic top on. I wonder why she chose that option when she planned this lesson... a fighting lesson of sorts.

"Aisling, if you can't manifest anything. Stop and go to the back of the line to watch your peers use theirs."

Frustration is building within me; I know I can use my power, but I've only been trying to manifest actual water. I've never used it away from it.

I close my eyes again and think back to what I had read in the books on water magic.

### *You can form weapons, Special One*

It's that voice, but I know by now that there isn't anyone in a physical form saying those words. It's in my mind.

But where is it coming from?

Is it my dead mother reaching me from the grave? She did call me her special girl, but the voice is different.

But the voice isn't wrong, I did read that whatever element you wield, you can use it to form weapons... only if you are strong enough and powerful enough.

I dig deep within myself and picture an icy sword. Nothing too fancy, just enough to use it in close combat. I would never strike Mrs Storm, although, she does deserve it.

I open my eyes to the feeling of ice seeping from my palms, and within moments I'm witnessing a sword being crafted before me. Once it's finished, I point it at the teacher. Showing her that I did it and could strike her within seconds. Would she have time to protect herself if I actually struck her with it? I don't dare find out.

"Well done, Aisling!" she gasps when she sees the sword in my hand.

"I've never seen another weapon wielder in my time! That is quite the gift." She beams at me, so excited for me or my power. I can't be sure but the entire class around me murmurs to the person next to them, and I'm standing here in shock.

"You are awesome! Why didn't you tell me you could do that?" Josh appears at my side.

"I didn't think I could." Still in shock, I let him take my arm and when my concentration draws away from the sword, it just disappears.

"I did that."

"You did," he reassures me.

# Chapter Eleven

"**Y**ou should have seen her! She was amazing!" Josh is still beaming after elemental class yesterday. I didn't get a chance to talk to Aylee last night back in our room. I wanted to do it without Neesh being there, but she retired to our room early. She said she wasn't feeling the best.

I know I still have to ask her about her thing with Josh. I don't even have the words for that right now.

"Really? Oh, I wish I could have seen it!" Aylee looks sad that she missed it but so happy to know I can wield such powerful magic.

"That would have been something to see," Neeshah chimes in. She's been very distant the last few weeks, I don't know what's gotten into her.

"Everything okay?" I ask her.

We are sitting near the oak tree in the courtyard. There are students wandering the halls and passing us by, none will look at us.

I wonder why.

"Yeah, just distracted. I know we have the final test

and award ceremony coming up, and I'm not prepared." She gets up from her seat and leaves me with Josh and Aylee.

"Okay, well you know we are here for you," Aylee calls after her.

"Do you know what's going on?" I feel as though I haven't been around much, I feel terrible. I've just been trying to focus on myself and growing my power. I know going into the "real world" is coming and I need to prepare myself for that.

"No, she won't even talk to me and I share every class with her." Aylee shrugs.

"Now that I have the two of you alone. Do you wanna tell me what's been happening?" I motion to the empty space between Josh and Aylee.

"What do you mean?" Aylee smiles at me sweetly.

"You know damn well what I'm talking about. Josh spilled the tea." Aylee whips her head around and narrows her eyes at Josh.

"I thought you would have told her, you two are best friends after all." Josh shrugs.

"We are, but I wanted to figure us out before I told her." She moves her hand back and forth between them.

"You know exactly what this is... we've done the research... now tell her." Josh tilts his head toward me.

"Fine," Aylee agrees.

"So..." I twiddle my thumbs together. This could go either way really.

"Josh and I are fated mates."

"Like, actually?" I know they told me they've done the research but fuck. My best friend has found her mate.

"Yeah, actually, it didn't click straightaway. There was an instant attraction of course, he's good-looking, but once our hands touched for that first time. It was instant. You just knew." Aylee looks at Josh admiringly.

"Well shit." My mouth is gaping open, my eyes are wide, and I'm in pure shock.

"I'm incredibly happy for you both! This is great news... will you tell the school?" Does the Academy even need to know?

"No, we are going to keep this as private as possible. Everyone can know we are a couple, but as far as fated mates. It's only going to be the three of us," Aylee tells me.

"Wait, three?" I pause. "Aren't you going to tell Neeshah?" I ask.

"No, it's a need-to-know basis and she's been off. We can't afford to tell her and have it get out."

"Fair enough, then your secret is safe with me." I open my arms and walk over to them both and wrap them up in a hug.

"Will you tell me more about being fated mates?" I release the hug and take my spot back.

"There's really not much to say, or to try to form the words to describe this feeling."

"I am so happy for you." I smile at them both.

"I really am. I wish nothing but the best for you both." I wonder if I have a mate out there for me.

I know it's not Gerrick, we would have felt that connection already, and we kissed too. Surely that would have sparked something.

"How are you and Gerrick going?" Aylee must have read my mind.

"Ah, I haven't seen him since sparring in the gym." I haven't heard from him since. He wasn't in our elemental class yesterday and I haven't seen him around campus. I wonder if he's been hiding in his room like last time, but I won't be going in search for him. I don't want him getting any wrong ideas of me... or us. The kiss with him was nice, but that's all it was... nice.

I didn't feel anything, I didn't get swept away or think I could die for that man. It was just a sweet kiss that was interrupted by a general... who happens to be his uncle. How fucking embarrassing.

He is so intense to be around, but oh so attractive.

The good looks must run in the family.

"I heard he's off the island and back with his father," Josh adds in.

"I didn't think we were allowed to leave until we actually graduated." This academy is like a boot camp for six months.

"He has special privileges. Having a general for a father and one for an uncle, the school allows this."

"Wow. I wonder if he'll be back in time for the test."

"Does it matter? He is the most skilled here and he has two older brothers who can look out for him." Josh sounds almost jealous.

"Okay, no need to get worked up about it." Aylee pats his shoulder in comfort.

"I'm going for a walk before dinner," I announce. I want to sneak off to the beach and practice my weapon wielding.

"You sure you don't want to stay? We are thinking of going to do more research at the library," she asks me.

"Yeah, I can do that this week after mythical class." I still haven't chosen a mythical Guardian to do my report on.

"Okay, we will save you a seat at dinner." She blows me a kiss when I walk away from the courtyard.

Fated mates...

Who would have guessed that?

I wonder how common it actually is, but the records don't show it.

Is it really that sacred?

* * *

At the beach, I managed to wield two ice swords, but my body was getting tired from draining so much energy.

I was hungry.

I enter the hall where we all eat together, and Aylee is waving me down. I walk toward them, and they are seated with... Gerrick.

What the fuck? I shoot Josh a confused look and he just shrugs.

"Fireball, it's nice to see you." He moves over a seat and lets me sit down next to him and Josh, sandwiched between the two. Aylee is directly across from me and I'm shooting her daggers.

"I wish I could say the same." He grabs his chest like I've stabbed him.

"That wounds my heart to hear you say that." He smirks at me.

The bastard.

"You're back," I say without glancing in his direction.

"I am, when father calls... you go running." He shrugs, like it's not a big deal.

"Okay." Is all I can muster.

"So, Josh here was telling me about how you can wield weapons." Gerrick raises his eyebrows.

"That's impressive, but can you actually fight with one?" That question catches me off guard.

Why would he ask me that?

"No... I mean I haven't actually tried to." I don't bother

mentioning that trying to hold the wield is hard enough without getting drained, let alone trying to use one in a fight.

"You should start practicing that." He turns away from me and focuses on the guy next to him.

"He isn't wrong, you know."

"How can I practice when no other weapon wielder is even here, Aylee?"

"Maybe you can ask Mrs. Storm to see if she can cast a spell to create the dummy to defend you with a magical sword too." That isn't a bad idea from Josh, but if I had to ask, it would have to be outside of class hours. I don't want any more attention to be drawn to me than there already is.

"I can just use my real one," Gerrick adds. He wasn't supposed to be listening in on our conversation.

"That would be pointless."

"Why would it? The enemy out there..." He points to the outside doors. "...won't be using magical weapons, they will be using real steel swords. You need to learn to fight against that." It's daunting to see how much knowledge he has of the outside world. The front lines of the war.

"I'm not asking you to do that."

"I wasn't offering on the whim you'd say no. Fireball, you will be doing it." Why is he helping me?

What's in it for him?

"Meet me in the courtyard tonight, when the moon is at its highest.

"Fine." I cross my arms over my chest, not liking my choice.

# Chapter Twelve

"I can come." Aylee stops me at our bedroom door. It's forbidden to leave our bedrooms after curfew. It's for our safety to remain in our rooms.

"No, it's going to be just like last time. I don't want you getting in trouble for me. This time he's training me... not going to harm me." I offer her a smile to convince her. I'm more trying to convince myself.

"Fine, but can you please come back as soon as your lesson is done... no fooling around." I nod my head and close our bedroom door behind me.

The hallway is eerily quiet. I have to adjust my eyes to the darkness and follow the pathway to the courtyard.

"There you are, Fireball. I didn't think you'd show." Gerrick steps toward me and away from the shadows.

"I still think this is a bad idea," I tell him, stepping close to where he stands. Trying to keep out of sight of anyone who dares break curfew.

"You need the practice and I want to spend any alone time I can with you. In my eyes, it's a win-win." He smirks at me. I can't believe I agreed to this,

"I know a place." I take his hand in mine and walk toward the little enclave that leads to my beach.

Having his warm hand in mine should send tingly feelings, but I feel nothing.

I wish that wasn't the case.


"Do you always sneak out of the wards?" Gerrick asks me when we are standing face-to-face on my beach. Yes, I've claimed it for myself. No one else comes here but me, and I'm in my little slice of heaven.

I wish I was here alone again, and I didn't have to share it with Gerrick, but we can't risk me using that much power inside the walls of the Academy, let alone risking harming a student... or him hurting me.

"I need this place to help me think." He nods, like he understands that.

"All right, let's see what you've got." He stands still with his sword in his hand. I inhale a breath and close my eyes.

I try to focus everything I have to wield a frozen sword, and when the rough, cold weighted sword forms in my hand, I open my eyes and look up to see Gerrick shocked. It's written all over his face.

"I didn't think it was true..."

"You just came out here on a whim?" Annoyance starts to grow.

"Well, yes and no. I heard every student from your class talk about it, but from hearing the tale to actually seeing it for myself, I didn't think it was true." He takes a step forward and examines the frozen design.

"What model did you use to create this?" He reaches out and traces the lines of the blade.

"I didn't, I just pictured a sword and this one appeared.

It's the same over and over. Nothing changes." It's almost like it's designed just for me, like my body knew it needed to craft this particular sword.

"It's stunning." I half smile at his compliment.

"Thanks, can we please try some moves? I don't have much time to hold the wield." I didn't want to have to tell him the truth, but if he is serious about training me, he needs to know.

"Okay, try bringing up the sword and swinging it against mine." Gerrick takes a step back and plants his feet solid on the ground.

He holds the sword at an angle, waiting for mine to make contact.

I close my eyes, praying, willing this sword to work in my favor.

My eyes open and I raise my sword above my head and strike against Gerrick's sword. There's a metal clash when they hit.

"Wow," Gerrick squeaks out.

"I didn't think that was going to work."

"Try not to think about your sword as ice, think it as if it's really a metal sword that can do damage. I think once you believe in your sword, you'd be able to wield it longer." He does have a point there.

"When did you become so wise?"

"When I started to... to fall for you." My breath hitches in my throat.

He did not just declare his feelings for me.

In the middle of a sword match.

Fuck.

"Again." He just continues like he never said anything, not a word...

I swing back the sword and hit his again.

"Again." I repeat the action, over and over until I'm out of breath.

"Stop," I say, breathless.

"I have no strength." And before our eyes, the sword disappears.

"Is that the longest you've held the wield?" Gerrick asks me, coming to sit beside me in the sand.

"Yes. I didn't think I could do it, but you were right about believing it to be a real sword." He smirks.

"Of course, I'm right." He nudges his shoulder with mine.

"Listen, about before... can we please pretend I didn't say anything." His gaze is out to the ocean.

"Sure, it's forgotten."

"Thanks." I stand up and offer my hand for him to take.

"We better get back before we get caught and I lose my slice of heaven."

"Good point." He takes it and stands beside me.

We walk back to the grounds of the courtyard in silence.

* * *

Back in the library, I'm trying to find any research on the Mythical Guardians to help me with choosing one for my report.

"Any luck?" Josh takes a seat next to me.

"No. I wish I knew a bit more on any one of them to make it easier to choose for the report." He takes a seat opposite me at the table.

"What is your gut telling you?"

"Nothing... I know you've chosen a griffin, but how did you come across that decision? How did you find any information about them?" I flip through all the books that have any mention of the mythical creatures, but they just tell me of their appearances and their respective nature.

"I'd heard folklore as a child, my parents and their parents before them all believed that the guardians are real." He can't be serious.

"I've never heard such stories."

"It is believed that the dragon rules them all, and if they misbehave, they were punished but never killed. You see, we need the balance of those Guardians to keep the realm of Inixiam alive. Otherwise, there will be no more magic." That part I believe, but it still doesn't make sense as to why there aren't any real records stating such stories.

"A dragon?" That's all my mind has gone to.

Can a dragon be so powerful to rule the other Guardians and our realm?

"Is there anywhere that you can... bond with a Guardian?" I know that is absolutely crazy talk, but we are Fae, we have powers, and we have fated mates... is it really far-fetched?

"I don't think so, they are a myth, after all." He lets out a laugh. I guess he is right. That would be so crazy to be bonded to a Guardian, imagine the power you would hold, wield, and the magic balance would be shifted.

"Just pick one and wing it. I know you'll do great. I'm late to meet up with Aylee." He gets up from his chair.

"Tell her I said hi, and I'll see her later." He nods and turns to walk out of the library.

A dragon?

Could that be for my project? I'm sure other students would have picked that one, let's go with something less obvious.

Like... a serpent.

That is more me, with the ocean... water theme.

I stare at my paper and begin writing everything I know and everything I believe to know about the serpent guardian.

It's been two hours since the first word landed on my page, and I think I've got a good report for Mr. Tomb.

I don't know why I always leave everything to the last minute, but I pack up my writing gear and put it away. I'm going to be late for mythical class and I finally can hand in this report.

"You were cutting it fine, Aisling... please take your seat." Mr. Tomb is standing at the door to his classroom.

"I hope everyone finished their report. We will be viewing each Guardian based on your findings." I take the empty seat next to Josh and pull out the report.

"Which one did you end up choosing?" Josh asks me.

"Serpent." I shrug my shoulders.

"Of course." He chuckles.

"What's so funny?" I hiss.

"Nothing, it's just the obvious choice for you, I always thought you would choose something out of your comfort zone."

"Well, if I didn't leave it to the last minute, I would have." I push my shoulder against his.

It's true though, I'm always the one pushing the boundaries.

"I see there are ten reports on the dragon, come on, guys. Do we really need that many on this one?" Mr. Tomb seems frustrated but bored.

"Ah, we only have one serpent and one griffin. Well done, Josh and Aisling." He smiles in our direction.

That comes as a shock since there are other water and

air wielders in this class... speaking of water...

Where is Gerrick?

I haven't seen him attend a single class since he's been back.

What is that boy doing?

"Let's go over those facts..." Mr. Tomb starts reading the facts and asking the students questions about their reports and I completely zone out.

*My eyes aren't my eyes...*

*I blink twice before they adjust to my surroundings.*

*There's a dark cave in front of me, and I hear very deep breathing, the air surrounding me is cold but I'm very warm, almost hot, but I'm used to it, like it belongs to me...*

"Aisling!" Mr. Tomb shouts my name. "Are you with us?"

I blink a few more times and I'm back in the classroom.

I turn to see Josh staring at me.

"Where did you go?" Concern is evident on his face, furrowed brows, and a thin line of his lips.

"I... I don't know."

"We've been trying to get your attention for five minutes straight," he tells me.

"That can't be right..." I look around the room, trying to get my focus back.

"Now that we have everyone's attention again, there will be only two more classes before your final test and the award ceremony. Make sure you pay attention and memorize everything you've learned these past five and a half months." He closes the book in front of him and that's our cue to leave.

# Chapter Thirteen

What happened to me in mythical class?

One minute I was listening to Mr. Tomb about dragons and the next I was in a cave somewhere, but I wasn't *me*.

I knew I had to talk to Aylee about this, maybe she can shed some rational information on it.

The steps to our dorm room feel heavy, it's like a dread consuming me or it's fear. It's *something* that's making me feel this way.

Our bedroom door is the two doors away from me on the left and I stop dead in my tracks when I see someone leaving.

It's not Aylee or Neeshah and it's certainly not Josh... I quickly hide in a break between rooms and peek around the corner.

It's .... Holy shit!

Micka! He doesn't teach any classes here, but he oversees the library and archives. I've never crossed paths with him yet, I know he can wield some lesser magic, as he's half

Fae and half *human*. I almost spit, it's uncommon for us to mix with humans, after all they are our enemy.

His power is knowledge. He can remember anything he reads and he's friendly enough.

They keep him here at the Academy, where it's safe for the both of us.

When I hear the footsteps descend away from this corridor, I make a quick walk to our room. I hope Aylee isn't too far behind to talk about this as well.

I open our door and quickly close the door behind me.

"Ash?" I spin around and find Neeshah, covering herself with her blanket, sitting in her unmade bed. I blink back the reaction of surprise and mask it with somewhat boredom. Hoping what I saw before is kept hidden away.

"I thought you were in class?" I ask her.

"I needed a break; I feel like I'm drowning here and needed to... clear my head." I nearly scoff. Yeah, like I believe that.

It's not only punishable to be fraternizing with staff here, but with a half Fae... that is punishable by death.

"Why aren't you in class?" She tilts her chin up at me.

"I'm finished for the day." That's not quite true, I have practice with Gerrick later. Chills run up and down my spine knowing I get to spend alone time with him.

Standing in the same spot I entered the room in, I sway back and forth... this is getting awkward.

"Tell Aylee I'm looking for her." I turn and leave the room. I don't think I can stand in here any longer.

What has happened to her?

The first four months here, it was great. Communication was on par, and now? It's like having a stranger staying with us.

I wonder how Aylee feels about this.

I also wonder what happened to her.

Walking down the dimly lit corridor, it feels sad knowing I'll be leaving soon. We all will be leaving soon, well, those who have passed the final test to graduate.

The steps leading to the courtyard crunch under my boots. I've grown used to wearing my fighting leathers everywhere, wearing my hair in a braided crown on top of my head. The only thing missing is my sword. I'm hoping once I graduate, I can visit the nearest town and get a blacksmith to craft one for me.

I scan the courtyard, hoping to find Gerrick here, maybe we can push training forward. I need a release.

I don't see him anywhere; I sigh in frustration. Maybe I don't need him, maybe I can try and wield something else to practice.

Turning on my heel, I walk to the enclave where it leads to my beach.

Reaching the bushes, I look over my shoulder and see no one else here. I walk right through and onto the sand beneath my boots.

Heaven.

The smell of the salt air, the coolness of the wind against my cheeks; I know this is where I belong, where I feel the most power. That and being outside of the wards. The Academy dampens our powers inside the walls, but once outside? It's all fair game.

"Should you be out here?" I feel the tingles spring to life inside my body before I hear his voice.

I spin around and see *him*.

General Dorian.

"I could ask the same thing about you," I taunt. I do have a death wish. He could haul my ass back inside and report me.

He could kill me here and no one would know.

I narrow my eyes, drinking him in. His fighting leathers hug every inch of his body, and I mean every inch.

His dark curly hair is pulled back into a tiny bun at the nape of his neck. His sword pokes out from the right side of his neck, it's sheathed on his back.

The fire pin is on his collar and a star sitting beside it. He graduated the Academy, that's what they give us students who pass, and the last pin I can't quiet see from here. Could it be his leadership pin? Army pin?

Who knows... and I don't dare ask him.

"Aisling, what are you doing out here?" He uses my name... the way it comes from his mouth does things. Things I don't want to think about.

"I'm practicing, I feel better by the ocean. Being locked up in there"—I tilt my chin to the walls—"makes my skin crawl most days."

"It's not safe out here." He takes a step toward me.

"I know the risks." I'm frozen in my spot.

"I don't think you do, the world... out here." He points to the ocean and beyond. "It's so fucking dangerous. That's why I'm here. I'm trying to bring awareness to it." He takes another step forward, like there's an invisible pull toward us.

"Yet, I still come out here. I belong out here, I'm not going to shy away from that."

"You should." Another step.

He is mere inches away from me, as he looks into my eyes, searching for something.

Dorian moves his hand toward me, inches away from my cheek. I inhale a quick breath. If I moved my face to the right, he would cradle it, but I don't. I'm still frozen in place.

He quickly drops his hand and the pain in his face is evident. He wants to touch me but is fighting the urge.

He takes a step back, giving us distance.

This isn't the distraction I was hoping to have.

"You can't be out here, it's not safe."

"You've said that already... there is something you aren't telling us, isn't there?"

"Yes."

"What is it?" It's like hot water has been thrown over me and I'm no longer frozen in my spot.

"There's been sightings of the Nurrigorgen near these shores. They are trying to find a way into the Academy, and if they see you out here. They will kill you."

"You've got to be fucking joking!" If they find a hole in the wall, they can easily break into the wards and kill each and every one of us.

"Shouldn't that have been your first priority? To warn the school?" I take a step back, why is he keeping this information to himself?

"I haven't been given orders to relay that message, Gerrick knows but has kept it to himself as well." Gerrick... what would he think if he saw me and General Dorian out here... together?

I squash that thought away and try to focus on this right now.

"We need to get back inside... now!" His eyes flare, his body turns rigid, he slowly reaches his arm above his head and withdraws his sword.

"What..." I begin to ask,

"Shh, when I tell you to run, you run for your life, Aisling." Dorian's gaze flicks to me again but turns his attention to behind me.

I don't dare look. I know in this moment I trust him completely.

"RUN!" he yells and he springs to life, running toward me and then past me.

I listen to him.

I run for my life and back to the inside of the wards. Where I am safe... for now.

My body slams into something hard, I'm sure I ran in the right direction.

"Oof," I say with a thud, strong arms grip my shoulders.

"Where are you going in a hurry?" I look up and see it's Gerrick standing here, holding on to me.

"I... ah..." Do I tell him?

"I was at the beach and Dorian... I mean General Dorian told me to run." It's not partially wrong, he did tell me to run but I won't tell Gerrick that he nearly put his hand to my cheek. A moment between us.

"What happened?" he asks, concern spreads right across his face.

"I don't know, all he told me was to run and he was running toward something, sword in hand." Danger. He was being the lethal warrior Fae everyone feared. He is a legend.

"I must go to him."

"NO!" I say loudly, I don't want him leaving me alone here or going into danger.

"I'm sure he can handle himself, please take me to my room." I would have fallen to the ground, but Gerrick's hands are still holding me up.

"Okay." He turns slightly, drops one arm, and wraps the other tightly around my shoulder. We walk together toward my room.

* * *

It's been two days since I was on that beach with Dorian.

I haven't been able to get Aylee alone to tell her what I saw the other day or what happened on that beach. It feels like forever since I've been able to talk to her. Neeshah is still sneaking around, and I know why. She's got a secret relationship. I do take offense that she hasn't told us; I thought we were her friends.

Sitting in the library, Josh plants a stack of books in front of me.

"What are these for?" I ask him when he takes a seat next to me.

"These are all the references I could find on dragons."

"Why do I need to know more about dragons?" I look at the stack of books, so confused. "I thought maybe we could gather some information on the enemy."

"What about the enemy?" I hold his gaze.

"Not today, we need to know all about the Mythical Guardians."

"That's not going to help us with the war outside those walls." I point to the bay window in the library, the large wall visible through the glass.

"I know, but it will help us graduate soon. To help past the tests, we need to know anything and everything about our classes and dragons are a huge part of that." He pushes the stack toward me, and I lift the top one off the stack.

*Dragon Lore* by Loriel the 100th scribe

I flip through the pages and my eyes land on a certain passage.

It reads:

*One who wields the most power can channel the power of the Guardians. It is believed that one's power will come from within, a certain Fae can control more than one element.*

*When that Fae learns to control more than one element, a guardian will choose that Fae to bond with.*

*A Fae who bonds a guardian will be granted immortal life and power.*

*It has only been recorded once, two thousand years ago.*

*The Griffin was fond of the Fae man, who could control three elements. His power was beyond what anyone could recognize...*

*His name was Arthur the Great.*

Chills run down my spine, how come we haven't learned about this in mythical class?

Is Arthur still alive if he is an immortal?

Only these books can give me that information.

# Chapter Fourteen

I skipped my last class and dinner to retire early to my room, I'm hoping I can speak with Aylee first before Neeshah gets to our room. I still haven't told her about the events from the last couple of days. I feel like since she found her mate, she's been too busy for me. I know that is selfish to say, as I've been busy myself, but even I spent time with Josh too... he is in all my classes.

I lie on my bed, daydreaming about the next two weeks. I'm sure they'll fly by and soon enough I can go to the war front lines and see my brother. I've missed him so much; I hope he's proud of who I've become here.

I do miss my sisters back home and Father, and I can't wait to see them soon. It'll be nice to just relax at home for a few days before heading along to my future.

I feel my eyes getting heavy and the comfort of my bed takes me to the land of dreams...

"Hey, Fireball." Gerrick's gaze burns into mine. He hovers over me on my bed. I feel the cool breeze against my naked skin and the feel of Gerrick's thighs between mine.

The way he's looking at me, touching me, is so erotic. I never thought I could have this kind of gentleness from him, let alone be in this position with him. I've thought about it, but never once did I think it would happen...

I close my eyes and feel the way his hand travels down my breasts, taking his time. I hitch in a breath when he pinches my nipple between his thumb and finger, and he just groans at my sound and the hardness of my nipple. Satisfied with my reaction, Gerrick's hand lowers farther down, moving his fingers over the curves of my hips, brushing his fingertips over my stomach and making his way down further south. They stop right above my sex.

I inhale a deep breath, waiting... anticipating his next move.

"Do you want more?" he asks me.

"Yes," I breathe.

His rough laugh vibrates in his throat, and I open my eyes to see him look down where his hand is. Like he's seeing art about to be made.

I feel his finger slide over my clit and down to my center.

My breath hitches when he plunges a finger inside.

"So wet for me, Fireball." I close my eyes and feel the warmth of his touch, my entire body alive from his finger.

"More."

He quickly pushes one more finger into my center and slowly begins to stroke in and out of me. I match his rhythm, lifting my hips to meet his thrusts. In and out, in and out.

I need to have more.

I want to feel more of him, this just isn't enough.

"Gerrick." The way his name leaves my lips, it's more of a plea.

His pace picks up with each moan I let out.

"Do you want to come on my hand or cock, Ash?" Gerrick kisses just below my earlobe before sucking it into his mouth.

"Cock," I moan out, the pace in his fingers just isn't enough.

"Please." I beg.

I look into his eyes, and I feel the vibration of his lips as he chuckles.

"Very well." He removes his fingers and positions over me.

I watch in awe as he grabs his cock in his hand, stroking it once, twice before he guides it to my entrance. I hold my breath as I watch him slowly push himself into me.

I groan at the sensation, the full thickness of him, I feel myself stretch around him.

"Sweetheart," Dorian groans. My eyes shoot open, and I see Dorian staring down at me, thrusting in and out.

In and out.

Dorian?

This can't be right.

The intensity of his thrusts begins to become harder and quicker; I can feel myself reaching my climax.

I don't have time to think, don't have time to move away, not that I want to...

I can feel my climax just around the corner.

In and out, Dorian thrusts are harder and faster.

"Sweetheart, come for me," Dorian groans out the words.

My toes curl in the bedsheets, and with the last thrust I scream Dorian's name.

. . .

I jolt awake, panting from my dream and I look around the room, hoping no one was here to witness myself orgasm to a dream.

But the room is empty. Thank fuck.

I don't think I could take that humiliation right now.

I was content dreaming about Gerrick having his way with me but Dorian? That... that was so unexpected. So... sexy...

He called me sweetheart, the way it sounded from his mouth, from those lips.

I shiver... it was only a dream.

The door flings open, walking side by side are Aylee and Neeshah. Talk about close timing.

"You here?" Aylee asks me. She takes a seat on her bed and Neesh takes the chair at the desk.

"Yeah, I." I clear my throat. "I wanted to get some rest before tomorrow." Elemental class is getting more intense, especially with the final test and graduation around the corner. Mrs. Storm wants us to be at our best.

"Understandable," Neeshah says.

"Where have you been lately? I feel like I haven't seen you at all these last few weeks." I turn to her, giving her my full attention. If she wasn't in class with Aylee every day, I'm sure she'd pick up on it.

"I, ah..."

"Don't lie to me, I saw someone sneaking out of our room, but I didn't want to say anything because I was expecting you to tell us... that's what friends do." I know I shouldn't have brought this up with Aylee in the room... unless she already knows and didn't tell me.

"You did?" She almost looks embarrassed.

"Yes, and don't worry, I haven't told anyone, well, except Aylee now... but that's beside the point. Neesh, I thought we were your friends, you know we don't judge... Hell, I just had a sex dream with Gerrick, and I have no idea where that came from." I guess I have to be semi-honest with her if I expect her to be open with us.

"Really?" Aylee adds in. I quickly turn to her and the expression on my face must tell her that this isn't the time to ask about this.

"It's okay, Neesh," I add in. Hoping I'm not pushing her too much on this.

"I'm sorry, I just thought if I kept it to myself then it wasn't a thing... you know?" She looks away.

"We promise," Aylee tells her.

"I'm seeing a librarian... but he's ah..." She hesitates for a split second, not sure how to say these next words. "He's half human." My eyes bulge, but I knew about him being at the Academy. Next to me, I hear Aylee inhale a sharp breath.

Half human, half Fae is frowned upon... like you could be killed on the spot if anyone found out, but I guess the Academy decided to keep him alive for his resources.

"What... the... fuck." I get those words out, trying to act surprised. Neeshah retracts a bit, shocked by the words from my mouth.

"I'm sorry, but can you please explain?"

"He is here, working, learning, and in exchange for his life, he helps in the library, working on the archives for us. I know he shouldn't be alive, but I am grateful that he is... I love him." Neeshah has a tear in her eye, like this man could really be what she wants.

"But that doesn't explain why." I can't help but want to get all the facts before I judge too harshly... or judge at all.

"He was born in Air Court, his mother was Fae... she died for loving a human. Micka's father is human and is also dead. He was a baby when a village family took him in. Once Lord Tatum knew of him, he made sure to come here, to the Academy to learn. And to be safe from those who would cause him harm and from the humans to use him as a weapon. He can use the smallest amount of magic but nothing like a full-born Fae can. That's why he's here, Micha is here to learn, to help us against the war with the humans." Wow.

I have no words.

"I never knew half Fae could exist in our world so peacefully. I wonder if there are more, they could also come here to be protected," Aylee thinks out loud. She isn't wrong, I am wondering the same thing.

It is highly frowned upon to have a human offspring but clearly not unheard of.

"I'm so glad you're safe and happy, Neeshah, I just wish you could have told us sooner." I get off the bed and Aylee follows.

I walk to where she sits on the desk chair and wrap my arms around her, Aylee follows suit.

"We love you too." Aylee laughs when she plants a kiss on Neeshah's forehead.

"Thanks." That's all she says.

# Chapter Fifteen

I'm jerked awake by the sounds of blustering alarms so loud they could burst my eardrums.

"What is going on?" As I squint around the darkness of our room, I can just make out both Aylee and Neeshah are putting on their fighting leathers.

"You need to get dressed now!" Aylee yells over the alarms.

I rip away the covers and jump out of bed. I locate my own fighting leathers and put them on. Tying up my boots, the two of them are already waiting at the door for me.

"What is going on?" I ask again but neither of them speak. We just run out the door and are suddenly surrounded by every student who is in our dorm block.

Terrified faces form a line to exit our dorms and enter the courtyard.

"Gerrick!" I call over the students talking amongst themselves; the loud alarm still going off.

He doesn't look my way; he mustn't be able to hear me. I don't try to make it over to him, there are too many students in between us.

"Have you seen Josh?" Aylee asks me, following me closely yet I have trouble hearing her words.

"No," I call out.

Neeshah is scanning the crowd, probably searching for Micka.

The teachers descend the stairs opposite us and meet us in the courtyard. There is no podium this time, so it's hard to see any of them, but they don't look happy. They even look scared.

"Students! Students!" Mr. Newett uses his powers to project his voice across the courtyard and everyone stops talking, stops moving, and they turn to where the teachers are standing.

Wide-eyed, we all wait for what he has to say.

"The reason for the alarms..." He inhales a deep breath, "There has been an attack on the Academy." Whispers and chatting start back up as scared students surround us. I can't believe it. I thought the wards are supposed to protect us from such attacks... yet it was easy for me to slip past them.

Shit. Did they find the weak spot?

Is this all my fault? I swallow the lump in my throat.

"We don't have all the details right now, but please find a weapon and be on high alert." Mr. Newett turns his back to us and talks amongst the other teachers.

"That's it? Just arm ourselves? Nothing about being defensive? Not split up into groups, just good luck?" I say to Aylee and Neeshah, but both their eyes are scanning the crowed.

I'm glad I don't have that instinct to try to find anyone.

I know Gerrick will be fine, he is a skilled warrior and I'm sure Dorian has already left the Academy.

So that just leaves, Aylee, Neeshah, and me... but those two have their focus elsewhere.

"I have to go find Josh!" Aylee's panicked voice calls out to me.

"I'll come with you, are you coming, Neesh?" I turn around and she's gone, without a word, just vanished.

What the fuck?

I turn around and shrug to Aylee, we will worry about her later. I don't think I can change Aylee's direction to search for Neeshah when Josh is all she is thinking about right now, and I get it; it's her mate. I think I would be there same too, but I don't have a mate. So, I don't know what that would truly feel like.

"Are you coming?" I snap my focus back onto the now and follow Aylee through the crowd. There are still a lot of students who remain in the courtyard, is it truly the safest place?

I don't think so.

"Josh!" Aylee calls out.

"Josh!" I start doing the same but there is no answer.

"Where was the last time you saw him?" I ask her.

Trying not to think the worst, but it's hard not too, he isn't here and everyone who goes to this academy is out here.

"We kissed goodbye before I went to our dorm. I should have watched him leave too, but I was just so tired." A tear slips down Aylee's cheek.

"It's going to be okay; we will find him." I don't dare promise her when I don't know the outcome.

If we have been invaded, there will be casualties.

What are they looking for?

Who are they looking for?

Why would they need to attack this place?

So many unanswered questions swirl in my mind. I can't focus. I just need to breath.

I stop.

I close my eyes and take a deep breath. Focus my mind and let it slip into nothingness.

My power vibrates through me, I can feel every electrical vibe through my veins, my skin, and that's when it clicks.

My eyes flutter open, and Aylee is crying harder now.

"Josh is near the infirmary." Her eyes snap to mine, tears slowing but still present.

I don't know how I did that but it's like my mind wanted to search for something, someone, and they just appeared.

Was I scrying?

That power is unheard of... and I've never trained that power...

**You can thank me later, Special One**

It's that voice...

I don't dwell long enough on it when Aylee takes off in the opposite direction and my feet carry me alongside her.

We get there in record time.

"Josh!" Aylee calls out once she pushes open the door.

She slumps to the floor, shaking.

"Aylee!" Josh calls back.

I let out a sigh of relief. He is here, and he's safe.

He takes Aylee into his arms and forces her to look at him.

"I'm here, my beautiful angel." He kisses the top of her head. Aylee sinks into the touch.

"Glad you're alive, Josh." I nod to him; he does the same back.

I finally take in the room before me and there are nurses running back and forth between rows and rows of beds.

"What the fuck happened?" So many beds, but they aren't empty. They are all full of people... with our people.

"The humans and their beasts attacked the library. We still don't know why or what they were looking for, but we have counted at least five dead." Josh swallows the lump in his throat.

"There are at least a dozen wounded. Ash, they are our friends, and we've lost two teachers." He pulls Aylee closer and inhales her scent, like he needed to be grounded again before he goes back to the wounded.

Josh gets up and takes Aylee with him. She composes herself and stares straight ahead.

"Is there anything I can do to help?" She turns to Josh, he just nods.

"You can help clean any wounds you see and bandage them up. It will be a day or two before our trained healers will get here." He swears under his breath. Like he knows that most of these people, in these beds before us, won't make it that long.

I get to work too; they don't need me out there. The threat has already left the island and now it's up to us to clean up their mess.

I walk over to one bed, the one closest to me on the left.

The cloth is already in the clean bucket of water, I reach in and wring it from the water and walk to the wound before me.

The stomach, the guts are hanging out from one side, and I close my eyes from the image, trying not to throw up.

This is fucking awful.

"Are they in pain?" I ask Josh when he walks behind me.

"No, Nurse Heyier has used a spell to take their pain away." That is truly a gift in itself.

"Guardians above," I murmur to myself. How can one heal from this type of injury?

"Try not to think, just let your hands do all the work." With that advice, Josh turns away and goes to where Aylee is already bandaging a fellow student. She always had the gentle touch with our kind and the land that surrounds us. I think that has something to do with her being from Earth Court. They always have been the kindest of the Fae.

I'm at my next bed when I see Rakie lying over one of the beds, sobbing. I walk up to her and touch her shoulder. When she moves out of the way that's when I see who she's crying for.

Rikie. Her twin brother.

He isn't breathing, he's lying so still.

"I'm so sorry," I murmur. There's not much I can do here so I continue on.

I'm up to my fourth bed when the door of the infirmary slams open and standing there is Neeshah. My eyes go wide.

She's still looking for Micka?

Her eyes scan the entire room, and she lets out a shaky breath.

"There you all are!" She closes the door behind her, gently this time. "Yes, we found Josh here and decided to remain and help out," I tell her.

"Did you find Micka?" Aylee asks her.

"No, I don't know where he is." She takes a seat in the empty chair beside an vacant bed, one that was taken only twenty minutes prior.

That student died from their injuries to their throat and chest.

Josh worked so hard to try and save them, but it was a losing battle.

"Micka?" Josh asks Aylee.

Oh! We haven't had the chance to tell Josh about what was going on with Neesh and her lover boy.

"It's a long story, but have you seen him? Did he help with the wounded here? He is a librarian." I relay part of the information to him and when he hears the title and his name... something inside of him just clicks.

His face stills, and his body goes rigid.

"What is it?" Aylee takes his hand in his.

"None of the librarians survived." His face is grim.

"No."

"No." Neeshah shakes her head.

"No! He was supposed to meet me." I drop the cloth into the water bucket on my way to her. She covers her face in her hands.

"Are you sure?" Aylee asks Josh.

"Yes, we have searched that library top and bottom for an hour now, and there are no more bodies to recover. I'm so sorry." He squeezes Aylee's hand.

"No, this can't be happening! I should have felt it! I should have felt that bond break! He has to be alive!!" I pull her hands away from her face and get her to look at me.

"What do you mean, you should have felt it?"

"She's bonded... I should have picked up on it, but I must have missed it." Aylee walks over to us.

I look between her and Neesh.

"I am... Micka is my mate, and I know I should have felt something if he died!" She abruptly gets up from the chair and stalks toward Josh.

"Show me." He just nods and they both walk away to the end of the room and to the only other door in the room. That's where they must keep the dead.

Maybe five minutes have passed, and they both emerge and Neesha is grinning from ear to ear.

"He's alive!!"

"Holy shit." Aylee grins in reply.

"But where is he?" I ask the obvious question.

"I don't know." Neeshah walks past us toward the door leading to the rest of the Academy.

"But I'm going to find out." She opens the door, looks back one more time, and that is our cue to follow her.

Well, shit.

# Chapter Sixteen

We race after Neeshah, down the hallways and corridors, before we reach the teachers' quarters.

"How do you know you will find them here?" I whisper to Neesh.

"Do you see any authority around? Do you see them putting the place back together or trying to re-ward the Academy? No, they are locked away in their war room and I demand to find out what the fuck happened here tonight." Aylee grabs on to my hand and squeezes.

"I know we said we would do this together, but I can't leave Josh." She leans down and kisses my cheek. She nods her regret to Neesh and backs away. I somehow get it, but then again, I don't.

"Looks like it's just you and me, water girl." Neeshah grins. I don't know where this rebellious side of her is coming from but somehow, I like it. I feel kinda badass right now too.

Instead of knocking, she pushes the door open, a bit

gentler this time than the infirmary, but she still forces her way in.

"Students," one of the teachers I don't recognize greets us.

"You both shouldn't be here," he continues to speak.

"Is Mr. Newett here?" Neeshah ignores him and asks a question herself.

"He's right in there." He takes a step back when he notices the flames pouring out of her hands.

"There's no need for violence," I murmur to her.

"Yes, there is. I need to know where Micka is." She moves past the teacher and toward the door at the end of the room.

We step under an enclave and see every teacher from the Academy and people we haven't seen before standing around a war map. It shows every island of the realm and intricate details of the Academy. I've never seen such a masterpiece. My entire body has come alive: the nerves in my body buzz and my eyes start to really take in the faces before us and when they land on a familiar face, my insides twist.

I can just make out him inhaling a sharp breath when he locks eyes with mine.

Dorian.

I thought he left. What is he doing here still?

"You shouldn't be here Neeshah Dryarit." Mrs. Storm is the one to address us, of course she would be one of the leaders in this room.

"Where is Micka!" she demands.

"I don't know who you are talking about," she responds back.

"Like hell you don't, he's the librarian... the only one

keeping this goddamn place going!" The embers in her hands are starting to glow again.

"Neeshah," I warn her. "We really don't want to get kicked out, when the final test and graduation are days away."

"You better listen to your friend." She turns back to talk amongst her colleagues.

"I asked you a fucking question." Her entire body is starting to glow with flames, red, orange, and a touch of light blue swirl all around her. How is this possible?

"That is enough!" Mrs. Storm shouts from across the room.

"I want answers! I will burn this fucking place down if I have to!" Neeshah looks them dead in the eyes.

She's serious.

The lengths she will go to find her mate.

I hope I never have to go through this, finding a mate... losing said mate... it just seems exhausting.

"I don't know what you want from us." Mr. Newett steps forward, hands in the air, palms up, facing us, showing us that he's not a threat.

"Lies! All fucking lies!! You know damn well who he is, and I want you to start telling me the truth!" She takes a step forward; I'm rooted in my spot. The flames are too hot to my skin, yet I know deep down they won't burn me. It's like a really warm blanket caressing my skin.

Strange, I'm a Water Fae, we should be afraid of the fire power, yet I stand here, inviting it in.

"Just tell her the truth, or I will." Dorian's deep voice breaks my trance on Neeshah's flame.

"Tell me what. At least someone is trying to do the right thing."

"Don't you dare! You don't have authority here." Mrs. Storm turns toward where Dorian stands.

"Not here I don't, but..." He jerks his chin toward the south walls. "...out there I do, and you will want that power on your side." He looks back to Neesh, her flames dancing around her body.

"Fine." Mrs. Storm, sags in her seat, defeated.

"Micka was kidnapped by the Eekyk." Confusion is evident on both our faces.

"They are the creatures those humans conjured up using our spell books and enchanted ornaments. They created hybrids. Those Eekyk are humans and birds mixed together." The distaste in her voice saying those words puts a foul taste in my own mouth.

"They flew over, knew exactly where our library was, and attacked it. If you've visited the infirmary, you'll know our casualties, and we know only Micka is missing. We assume they've taken him."

"Where?" Neesh demands.

"We don't know, that is the only information we have right now." I look toward Dorian, hoping he might have more to give us, but he looks as defeated as we feel.

"The final test and graduation will remain; we are not postponing it. So you two best be off and get some sleep. You have a very busy schedule this week." Mr. Newett walks toward us, shooing us with his hands and closes the door behind us.

"Kidnapped!!" Neeshah turns to me, tears swelling in her eyes. I wish there were words I could say to make her feel better, but I've come up empty.

"I'm sorry," is all I can muster up.

* * *

The next morning, every student is weary and extremely tired but as Mr. Newett said last night, we don't have time to wallow away and do nothing. We have to study, prepare, hope, and pray to the Guardians that we pass graduation.

"What a night!" Gerrick matches his pace with mine, resting an arm across my shoulders.

"Where were you?" I hiss at him. I went looking for him, but he was nowhere to be seen.

"I, ah... had something to do." He doesn't look at me, it's like he's hiding something from me.

"I thought we said no more secrets..." I stop, he follows suit, and we stand facing each other. I cross my arms over my chest.

"Fireball, you said no more secrets. I never agreed to such things." What an ass!

I turn from him and walk away. I don't need his energy seeping into me today.

Today, is a sad day. One we all will remember for a lifetime; the burial of our fallen brothers and sisters.

# Chapter Seventeen

"Can you believe it's two days to go?" Aylee walks alongside me to enter the breakfast hall.

"I don't, I honestly don't even want to think about it." The stress of everything is building up inside me, yearning to burst its way out.

"Have you spoken to Gerrick?" She knows the tension between us, but the truth is, I don't mind the space either... especially, since after having another erotic dream about him and then it morphed into a dream about Dorian.

"Did you hear?" A panting Neeshah rushes up to our side. We give her a confused look.

"The Fire Lord Killian is making an appearance at the Academy today." Holy shit, what could that mean?

"Formation, students!" Mr. Rowenfield calls before us. We all scurry to our power quadrant.

"I am pleased to inform you that we have Fire Lord Killian here today." He gestures to the man standing next to him.

Holy shit.

He's attractive.

My head turns in Gerrick's direction when he scoffs.

"What?" I ask him.

"Nothing," he spits out.

Lord Killian steps forward to address us.

"You may have heard many rumors or speculation about myself needing a wife... a woman to become Lady of Fire Court, well I am here today to tell you that those words... are indeed true." Everyone around me is murmuring, whispering amongst themselves.

What does that mean?

Will he choose one of us, or do we volunteer? I take a small step backward. I have no interest in becoming a bride.

I would rather be on the front lines with my brother.

"I'm sure you all have many questions, but the most unanswered one would be... do I choose?" He looks at everyone in the crowd and his eyes light up when he spots *me*.

"The answer is, yes. I will choose one of you to become my wife." He beams with pure joy.

"That's it, students, back to classes," Mr. Rowenfield instructs us.

I break away from Water formation to find Aylee on the same track in finding me.

"Can you believe that?" she asks me when she's finally reached me.

"No, but honestly I'm starting to believe anything right about now," I dryly say back.

"You think he will actually choose someone from here?" Neeshah comes up from behind us and chimes in.

"It's possible."

"Well, out of the three of us, you are the only single one left." Aylee laughs.

I roll my eyes. "How's the search going for Micka?" I ask Neesh, trying to change the subject.

Am I single? Do I have something going on with Gerrick? I haven't really spoken to him in the last couple of days, he's been extremely distant, and then those dreams with Dorian... I don't know what to think anymore.

All I know is, I don't want to be the one chosen.

Can you picture it, *me* a Lady of Fire Court? I scoff at the idea.

"It's at a standstill! This fucking Academy won't let me do anything. They've deemed the 'outside' world dangerous and that I should let the professionals deal with it." She air quotes the word outside.

"The Fae warriors are the best; you should trust them." I know one in particular who is the best of the best... Dorian.

"That's bullshit and you know it!" Neesh stomps her right foot into the ground, a little cranky.

"I don't, you know the protocols."

"Again, that's bullshit. I should be out there trying to find him!" she huffs in frustration.

"If you go out there unprepared, you will die. Do you honestly want that? Would Micka want that?" I know it was a low blow using Micka as an excuse, but I know I'm right and she will too.

"No, he would want me safe..." She drops her gaze. Defeated.

"Good, I'm glad we reached that conclusion, now I'll see you guys after class," I say to the both of them and walk away.

Shaking off the negative talk, I'm going right into the devil's den... combat class.

I push open the doors to the gym, inhaling the scent of sweat, leather, and musk with a tinge of amber. Strange.

I look around the room, I don't see anything out of the ordinary. There are the same classmates, the fighting mats, and our teacher, Mr. Rowenfield. I don't see Gerrick anywhere, my heart drops. I wish he was here, maybe I could get him on the mat and we could spar out our differences.

Try to find what the problem could be, one minute he was all hot and then next completely cold. I don't do on and off. I'll give him a chance to explain himself, but I'm out. Done.

I can feel the invisible walls around my heart start to build back up, and if I'm being completely honest with myself, I don't need emotional baggage going into war. I want to be the only person on my list. No one else.

Anyone else on that list could get me killed.

### Smart, Special One

It's that voice again, I didn't think I would hear it again.

There's something comforting about it, it's like I'm not completely alone with my thoughts. That there is someone out there looking out for me, watching me and a little bit of cheering me on. I like it.

At first, I was scared, worried, but now? I'm happy it's there.

My little cheerleader.

### I'm anything but little...

The voice replies, my lips twitch at the little snip.

Okay, noted.

"Does anyone want to go first?" Mr. Rowenfield asks his

students before him. I know I have been practicing but I'm nowhere near good enough to actually go first.

"How about I give them a lesson today?" Lord Killian steps out from the shadows.

Holy shit.

He looked beautiful up on the podium before, but up close and personally, he is breathtaking.

His black hair is short, showing off the point of his ears, his mysterious dark but amber eyes shine bright in the gym lights. His half smirk, keeping secrets hidden.

The clothes he wears are of high standing, of course they have to be, he is a Lord, but they reflect expensive taste.

He doesn't wear anything royal like he should, instead he wears fighting leathers, but it shows off his standing in the Fire Court.

A Fire pin at his collar and there's another one I can't make out what it represents.

"Are you sure?" Mr. Rowenfield asks, confused. I take it that he was only supposed to watch.

"Of course, if they are to fight in the Fire Court army, I need to know they won't die on their first day. It would be a shame." His smirk doesn't falter.

He's enjoying this.

"Who would you like to spar with?" my teacher asks.

"You pick your best fighter, and then your worst." I swallow the large lump that quicky formed in my throat.

Shit.

I'm the worst fighter.

No... no... this can't be happening.

Fuck.

I watch in horror as Trent walks up to the mat and faces Lord Killian.

The Lord has a few inches of height compared to Trent and the muscles... he's been training, and it shows.

Both of their stances are ready for an attack, but Lord Killian is the one to make the first move.

He races toward Trent, but he is too quick, he dodges the first punch. Trent composes himself and strikes Lord Killian with a combination attack, fist and kick. Lord Killian could only dodge the first but mistakenly gets kicked in the side. He groans from the impact.

"Very nice," Lord Killian praises Trent.

Standing up straight, they face each other once more but Lord Killian is ready to attack again, however Trent wasn't fast enough this time. He lands a hard blow to Trent's jaw. It knocks him down and he remains on the mat.

"You fought well, Trent; I can see why you're the best in the class." Lord Killian offers him a hand and Trent takes it.

"All right, Aisling. You're up next," Mr. Rowenfield calls.

Fuck.

"You've got this!" a girl calls from my left. I smile weakly at her.

This will be over in a second, especially how Trent went down without Lord Killian breaking a sweat.

"Pleasure to meet you, Aisling." Lord Killian sweeps a low bow upon greeting me on the mat.

A gentleman.

"Let's get this over with," I huff in frustration.

So many thoughts run through my head, like why am I the one to be chosen to fight against a Lord... of all people?

Why do I have to be the worst in the class to be presented this opportunity to fail... again?

"Aisling?" Lord Killian calls my name.

"Sorry," I murmur.

"Are you ready?" he asks me.

"Ready as I'll ever be."

Fuck it.

I race toward the Lord, hoping to catch him off guard, but he sees me advance and dodges my first punch. Lord Killian isn't surprised at all; he grabs my arm and gives me a hard but gentle push away from him.

I compose myself and try to advance again, but this time I pretend to punch him in the face, instead I swing my elbow out and get him square in the ribs. He grabs his side. I take the chance and whirl around and kick him behind the knee, it knocks him to the ground.

I don't waste any time, I wrap my right arm around his throat in a headlock.

"Do you yield?" I ask him, but he doesn't say anything.

I ask again, "Do you yield?"

"Yes." He taps my hand and I release him.

He stands up straight, takes a step away from me, and turns around.

His face radiates appreciation and pride.

"You did well, and yet you are supposed to be the worst in the class." Lord Killian cocks his head.

"Yes, well, I think you just let me win."

"I assure you, I did not." He bows before me and exits the room.

I can't believe I took down Lord Killian...

Me?

# Chapter Eighteen

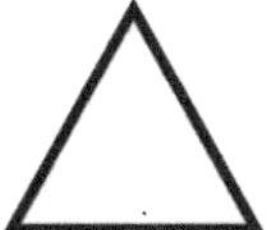

"You did WHAT?" Neeshah asks in horror.

"I took down Lord Killian on the sparring mat today."

"You didn't... you of all people," Neeshah retorts.

"What is that supposed to mean?" I snap. I turn to her, staring straight into her narrowed slitted eyes. My eyebrows draw together in anger.

"Well, it's not like you're the best fighter. At books, yes, but not on the mat. We all know that." She shrugs.

"Today was different!" I turn my back to her and walk out of our room. I leave Aylee open-mouthed on her bed.

I need some fresh air.

Today was different. Standing on that mat facing Lord Killian, I felt a surge of energy I haven't felt before. It was almost hot, like flames caressed my entire body, but never actually there to burn my skin... it was almost like it was *inside* of me.

My feet are carrying me to my favorite spot at the Academy. Along the shoreline, not where I'm supposed to be but where I'm needed.

"You shouldn't be here." Gerrick steps out from the shadows, I nearly didn't recognize him, but his scent filled my nose, leather and salt. It makes sense since he is a water wielder.

"I could say the same thing about you." My hands land on my hips, fighting the urge to turn around and walk away from him.

"I... ah... needed a minute to myself. Especially for the next two days." Shit. I almost completely forgot.

Tomorrow is test day, and the next is graduation.

Then we are out into the world as trained warriors.

He takes a step closer to me, his eyes darken, and a smirk rises on those perfect lips.

"I'm glad you're here, Fireball." He takes another step toward me. "I think a redo kiss is needed; don't you think?" He closes the distance between us and my breath hitches in my throat.

"No, I don't think so." I push at his chest, but he doesn't move.

"Are you sure?" His tongue darts out and licks the bottom of his lip. My eyes follow the action, doing the same unwillingly.

"Yes," I breathe.

"Your body is telling me something different." He grins.

Fucking grins!

My body is reacting to him, but my mind is screaming to tell him to fuck right off.

His hand reaches out and traces the line of my jaw, to my chin, and back to the other side of my jaw.

I shiver at his soft touch.

"NO!" I push him away, harder this time, and he steps away.

"What's wrong?" he asks me.

"You have no idea, do you?" I take another step away from him, fury radiating my body.

"I asked, didn't I?"

"You've been hot and cold with me. One minute we are making out and let's be honest, it was hot. And the next minute, you are so cold toward me, it's like I'm in Winter Court!" I shout at him.

"What is it, Gerrick? Are we hot or are we cold?" I narrow my eyes at him. At this point, I don't care what his answer is, I've already made up my mind.

Cold.

"Fireball... baby... Ash," he stumbles, not convinced of any cute nickname he gives me.

"I'll tell you, cold. That's what we are. After graduation, we will be stationed at different posts in different Courts, so it's best we just end whatever." I motion back and forth between us with my hand. "This ends here and now." I nod my head at him and turn my back and walk down the shoreline. Feeling my power surge within my body, my blood, and nerves, I need to let it out.

My feet stop just mere inches away from the shoreline, the waves coating the sand, back and forth. I close my eyes, raise my hands up in front of me, and I scream so loud I'm sure anyone close enough within the wards can hear me, but I let it all out. The ocean waves become angry, splashing hard against each other, raising higher and higher.

I open my eyes and see the waves so high above the ground, they are still. Not a drop of water touches the ground. It's an amazing sight.

I feel the heat rise within me again and there are no words to describe this feeling. It's my power but I know the feeling of water, the smoothness of it, the slight chill when it finally surfaces but with this heat. It's wild, uncontrollable... it's different but it feels so good.

I tilt my head up at the moon, shining down on me and I close my eyes. Wishing I was somewhere else, somewhere safe and wrapped up in familiarity. I open my eyes and decide to head back to bed. I need as much sleep as I can before test day tomorrow.

I need to pass, my future rides on it.

* * *

One more test to complete, one more test before I pass and it's fucking combat.

I groan out loud, but no one is standing beside me to hear it, they've all gone to watch Gerrick and Josh spar. There is no rule that if you lose the match, you fail. It's how well you perform on the mat that determines if you pass or not.

I have passed all my written assessments, and my weaponry test. I knew I would, but this last one... I'm not so sure.

But as I stand here, watching a couple of the students sparring for their lives, I know I'm in trouble. They give everything to the fight, trying to show their worth, that they deserve to be here and to graduate tomorrow.

If you fail more than two written tests and lose the sparring match, then you don't graduate... you fail.

You either get the option to repeat another six months or to return home and try again in a year... or two... or never. The choice is yours at the end of the day, but no one wants to fail and return home a failure.

I sure as hell won't.

I couldn't face my father, let alone sending a letter to my

brother that I wouldn't be joining him... he would be so disappointed.

His words are as plain as day... "I taught you everything I knew and yet you still failed. I guess I trained you for nothing, Ash." I let out another groan and Aylee steps up next to me, bumping her shoulder against mine.

"You're going to be fine," she says.

"You have more faith in me than I do," I say dryly.

"Don't sell yourself short, Ash, you did beat Lord Killian." She smiles.

Yeah, no idea how I managed that. Maybe he let me win?

But if I hadn't, then I wouldn't have been worthy to even take the grand tests today... so, what was his point? If he let me win...

"Ash, and..." Mr. Rowenfield pauses and looks down at his list, my stomach drops when he calls, "Aylee."

Fuck.

I turn my head and see her smile drop almost instantly.

"I'm so sorry," she whispers as she takes a step away from me.

How can I fight my best friend? How is that fair?

Now I'm glad that if either one of us lost, we can still graduate, it's based on a collective score. That doesn't mean I want to fight her. She is incredible on the mat.

I inhale a deep breath and follow her to the empty blue mat in front of us. The students standing around, separate, letting the two of us pass and step onto the mat. Facing each other, I smile weakly.

"Let's get this over with."

# Chapter Nineteen

Graduation.

That bittersweet word.

I made it.

"Are you ready?" Aylee comes up behind me while I'm checking myself out in the mirror.

Making sure my fighting leathers are secured and my hair braided is neatly tied on the top of my head in the formation of a crown.

I look at her from the reflection of the mirror, I cringe when the black eye is already starting to turn purple.

"I am so sorry about that." I nod toward the eye.

"Don't worry about it, it was a good hit and it won you the match." She smiles then grimaces in pain.

"That doesn't mean I don't feel shit about it." She comes to stand behind me, placing her hand on my shoulder.

"I've never been prouder of you than in that moment, Ash." She smiles again at me and squeezes my shoulder.

"Where is Neesh?" I haven't seen her at all these last two days.

Did she take the test? If she did, did she pass?

Is she going to be there at graduation?

So many questions floating around, and I'm not sure they will get answered until I see her.

"I have no idea, I thought you might have seen her." She turns away from me and goes to stand at the end of Neesha's bed.

"It doesn't look slept in."

"I'm worried about her; you didn't see her when she interrogated the teachers. She was—"

"I was what?" The door swings open and there standing in the doorway is Neeshah.

"Nothing…" I step away from the mirror and turn to see her for the first time in two days.

"No, finish what you were going to say." She doesn't move, just glares at me from across the room.

"I was just saying how we haven't seen you in a few days."

"You're lying." She crosses her arms over her chest.

"She's not, but we are allowed to worry about you. Ever since Micka was kidnapped, you haven't been the same." Aylee steps in, coming to my aid.

"Would you be the same if it was Josh?" she quips.

"No, but that's not…"

"The same?" Neesh finishes for Aylee.

"But it is though, he's my *mate* and Josh is yours. It's the same." Neesh gives us both a once-over and then turns on her heel to leave the doorway behind.

"What was that about?" I look over at Aylee but she just shrugs.

"Come on, we better get going or we will be late for graduation." Aylee squeals. I can't help but share her excitement.

Today is the last day at the Academy and I'm so excited

to finally see my brother.

"Congratulations, Aylee, you've completed the six-month training at the Academy of Elements." Mr. Rowenfield holds out his hand for her to shake and presses the gold star to her collar, representing the completion of the Academy training.

Josh cheers his excitement next to me at his mate graduating.

I share his level of cheers and I don't see Neeshah anywhere. I thought she would be here with us.

Aylee takes the steps down from the podium and makes her way back to us.

"That was exhilarating!" Aylee quietly says to us when she reaches us.

"You looked amazing up there." Josh leans down and kisses her forehead.

"I can't wait until you're up there, Josh, I've never been more proud of you." Aylee beams at her mate.

The empty feeling starts to sink into my bones. I don't have anyone like that here to cheer me on. I know that is silly to think but I can't help it. I know I have Aylee's and Josh's friendship and I wouldn't wish that away, but it's just the loving... feeling I'm missing.

"Where is Neesh?" Aylee turns to me and asks.

I shrug.

I thought since leaving the dorm she would be here, but I scan the crowd and I can't seem to find her anywhere.

"That is so strange!" Aylee does the same and scans the crowd.

"Oh well, it's her loss if she doesn't want to be here; she doesn't get to graduate. I wonder what she will do instead..." Josh trails off when his name is called up to the podium.

"I love you." Aylee mouths to Josh when he turns away from us.

"This is exciting!" She beams again.

I'm a ball of nerves because I'm next after Josh.

He takes the steps and walks toward Mr. Rowenfield.

"Congratulations, Josh, you have officially graduated from the Academy of Elements, I wish you nothing but the best of luck for the world outside these walls. You are one hell of a warrior." I feel one heated tear slip down my cheek.

This will be officially the last time we are all going to be in one room together, and I don't want it to end.

I know there isn't anything I can do to try and keep us together, and I know I can't try and get us stationed at the same frontline camps.

Josh shakes his hand and takes his star badge and descends the stairs.

Aylee rushes over to him and jumps into his arms, he catches her without faulting.

"You both look good, warriors." I smile.

They are so fierce, so in love, and dangerous. I love that.

"Aisling." My head whips to the podium.

My name has been called.

This is it.

I give Aylee and Josh one more glance and walk toward the podium where all the professors, teachers, and mentors are standing.

This is it.

I'm going to get my badge of honor and officially become a warrior.

I never thought this day would come.

If anyone deserves this, it's me.

"Congratulations, Aisling, you have become one of the finest warriors I have had the privilege of teaching." Mr. Rowenfield hands me the star.

"I hope the Guardians are watching over you, you are a special one, Aisling. Use your power for good." He shakes my hand, I start to walk away, tears flowing freely down my cheeks when I stop at the sound of someone clearing their throat.

I stop.

I turn around and see Lord Killian standing in front of everyone.

"Do you have something to say?" Mr. Rowenfield asks him, impatience in his tone. He'd better be careful of how he talks to a Lord.

"I do indeed." He clears his throat again and addresses everyone here.

"As you all know, I came to this Academy to find a wife. Someone who will become the next Lady of Fire Court, someone who can stand beside me and rule our court. I have in fact found someone... here at the Academy and it is my pleasure that my chosen wife is...

Aisling!" My brows shoot up. My world spinning on its axis.

This can't be right.

The entire student body is gasping and talking amongst themselves.

Lord Killian turns to me, addressing me alone.

"You have shown strength, knowledge, and great power being at this academy, and I wouldn't want anyone else to become my wife." He takes a step toward me.

This can't be happening.

"No," I whisper.

"You can't refuse a Lord," Lord Killian says back with a steady voice.

I gain the tiniest bit of confidence and red-hot flames lick around my blood.

"I can't be your wife!" I say.

"Are you spoken for?" He asks me.

"No, I—"

He cuts me off, "Are you mated with anyone?"

"No," I deadpan.

"Then you are to be my wife, I will pick you up at your family's home after the graduation break." He takes a step back and pivots.

He walks away from me and the rest of the Academy, who are all staring at me with wide expressions.

Shock.

Dismay.

Happiness

Even jealousy is there.

Fuck.

I've just sold my soul to a Lord.

# Chapter Twenty

"**I** can't believe you get to marry the Lord of Fire!" Aylee beams, trying to get my mood up.

This isn't working.

"I don't want to be married off! I want to be there on the front lines like the warrior I've trained so hard to be! This is so fucking wrong." Packing my bag, every student at the Academy now has leave to spend time with their family before they get shipped off to the stations. I was hoping I could spend a day with my family back home and then travel to be with my brother, hoping the general where he's stationed would let me stay to prove that I'm an asset.

But now my plans have completely changed... for the worse.

"Don't be like that, Ash, you've been given a blessing." She tries to find any positive in this.

"How? I feel like I've been given a death sentence." I collapse on the bed when my one bag is packed.

"You will be clean, smelling of fresh flowers, and get dressed up in lavish gowns. You get to plan balls, attend charity meetings, and maybe he might even let you in on his court business." She shrugs. She sure knows a lot about what happens at court.

"I doubt it, I think I'm going to be his *pet,*" I spit out that last word.

"Don't be like that. This is an opportunity of a lifetime; you get to live a long and healthy life. You could die on the battlefield the first day you are assigned." She scrunches up her face at the thought. That is her reality.

"That... that is the life I want. I want to be a fucking warrior!!" I shout the words, the power surging in my veins awakening.

"Calm down, just think... with the amount of power and resources at your fingertips, you might be able to find out what happened to your mother and sister that night..." She never brings up my family like that, but she has a point... maybe I can get some answers now. I wonder if Lord Killian will allow me to do so.

I smile.

The first smile in the twenty-four hours since I've graduated.

"There's my Ash." Aylee comes over and taps my knee.

"So, do we know where Neeshah went?" I ask her.

When we returned to our dorms last night, the room was empty, her bed was neatly made, and all her belongings gone.

She left.

But where did she go?

"I heard she ran off to go back home, she was embarrassed to graduate." Aylee shrugs, she doesn't seem to care too much.

"That doesn't sound like her."

"Maybe the professors killed her and tossed her body in the ocean." Aylee sits down at the end of the bed.

"That isn't believable either. No way would they kill a potentially powerful Fae." Fire is probably the most powerful power on the island.

"That's true, I don't know where she went or why, but I do know that it was her choice and I've made peace with that." She stands, grabs her pack, and heads for the door.

"Will you spend time with Josh before going to your parents?" I ask her. Things are more complicated for her now, but I'm glad she doesn't have to spend more than a few days with her parents. As much as they are caring... they are over-the-top... they didn't want her to become a warrior. They wanted her to stay in the village and marry the farmer boy. She was against that, and that's why we came here.

"Yeah, we have planned to visit his family first and he agreed to come meet mine." The pure joy in her face is contagious and I smile along with her. Knowing that makes my future dread disappear for a little while.

"You are going to be fine, Ash. You are a survivor." She blows me a kiss and walks out of our dorm one last time.

I take a moment in the silence to reflect everything that has happened in the last six months.

Falling for a boy.

Being the best fighter I can be.

Honing my power.

Meeting new friends and dealing with death.

Graduating and now becoming a Lady of Fire Court.

How is this my life?

I never wanted any of it.

All I wanted was to graduate and reunite with my brother.

He's the only one who understands me, gets me, and my only family if I'm being completely honest with myself.

* * *

"You're home!" My father races out the door of our home and wraps me in his arms.

The smell of pine leaves and ash fill my nose.

It's the smell of home.

Not my home.

"Hi, Father," I murmur.

"Your sisters are eager to see you too. Why don't you let me take that?" He tries to grab my pack, but I refuse him.

"No, I can carry it." I pull it from his grip.

"Okay." He drops his gaze to the ground but doesn't argue.

"Why don't you come in, your room is exactly how you left it." Of course, it is. That is the only thing in this entire house that would remain the same.

Ever since my mother was killed, it was his mission to change everything about the house we have lived in for our entire lives. But yet, he didn't dare change my room while I was gone.

"How are my sisters?" I ask him, following him into the living room.

Looking around the dull room, the only light coming from the two small windows on the far east walls and the small lit fire in the fireplace.

"They should be arriving home shortly." I turn to look at him, confused as to why they aren't already home, and where they could be.

"The girls are in town fetching fresh meats and vegetables. We are to have a feast tonight in celebration of your achievements." I wonder what he's referring to.

Would it be the Academy?

Or would it be my nuptials to Lord Killian.

I nod my head and turn on my heel. A nap would be the best solution right now. I need to rest after my long journey home and before my dear sisters' arrival. They will have plenty of questions, and when I give my answers, there will be more questions... it's a never-ending cycle.

It's brutal.

# Chapter Twenty-One

"You're here!" Violet screeches when she steps inside the front door.

My two other sisters follow behind her, but they don't say or look at me. That's not like them.

"Here I am," I say sarcastically.

"How was the Academy?" Kourt asks me.

"It was challenging, but worth it, Alec was right. I learned so much." I smile, the only true smile I've done since being back home.

"What did you learn about?" Terreasa asks, she walks down the corridor toward the kitchen.

Mary, our cook, will prepare dinner for us.

I'm surprised Father can still afford some staff to remain at the house after what happened with mother and Lord Marcus.

"Plenty, the history of the realm was so fascinating." I take a seat in the living room when Kourt disappears with the basket of food for the kitchen.

"Were there any boys?" Violet asks.

"There is no need to answer that, Aisling." Father's voice echoes around the corner.

I wonder how much he heard.

"It was a mixed school; you should already know that." I shrug my shoulders, not wanting to give off any clue on what happened there... or what didn't happen.

I wonder what Gerrick is doing. I didn't see him at graduation, maybe he got a private ceremony for whatever reason.

"Surely there was a boy!" Kourt says as she walks back into the living room, catching onto our conversation.

"Enough," Father says.

"We have more important matters to discuss than a boy your sister may or may not have been involved with." I'm shocked Father is sticking up for me. This isn't like him.

He has always sided with my sisters over me.

"Important matters?" I query Father.

"Yes, you graduated from the Academy, which means you'll be receiving a letter soon to where you'll be stationed. I wonder if you'll get the same outpost as your brother. Has he heard the news?" My heart skips a beat. He doesn't know about Lord Killian's proposal.

"I hope so," I murmur. I know I won't, my fate is already sealed by another.

"Where is Emmie?" I ask Father, she hasn't been mentioned since I've returned home. I thought she would have been brought here to be with us all.

"In her room, she is quiet most days."

"Is everything okay?" I ask, concern edging my tone.

"She's fine, she doesn't want to see anyone..." Maybe I should visit her in her room, I've always been her favorite even before her "accident." That's what we call her situation, no one wants to talk about Mother's murder and Emmie's accident.

That is something I hope to try and solve while in Fire Court. I could find my time useful there. It's whether Lord Killian will allow it or not.

"Can we go back to talking about boys?" Violet asks.

"No, there is more to life than boys, Daughter." Father's tone is clipped. Surely this topic would come up every now and again since he did have five daughters and only one son. We all have to marry someday, maybe I should be the one to talk about their futures?

Without giving myself away in the process, I want to keep my secret a secret for as long as possible.

"Maybe it's time to discuss their futures, Father." I shrug, not wanting to make eye contact with anyone.

"Do you think being back less than a day, you have the right to bring up and 'discuss' their futures?" he hisses.

"You don't have the capability to talk about their futures or make decisions. Brother and I had to do that for ourselves. I think being home is the right time to talk about it." My voice gets louder, trying to get the point across.

"It doesn't concern you." Father stands from his spot, glares at me, and exits the living room.

I huff out my response.

"Thanks for trying," Terreasa murmurs.

"Do any of you want to go to the Academy?" I ask, not even sure if any of them have manifested their powers yet.

"None of us want to go," Violet chimes in.

"Why?"

"We... don't have powers like you and Brother have. We will be happy with the life Mother and Father had. Getting married, supporting our husbands, and having kids." I think about that for a moment, what it would have been like if I had chosen that pathway... but it quickly vanishes. I wasn't born to be a housewife, not like there's anything wrong with that, it's just not for me.

"But you could have so much more, see so much more," I tell them.

"That's not the life we have chosen. Kourt already has a suitor lined up." My head whips around to Kourt and she just shrugs, like it's not a big deal.

"When did this happen? What has Father said?" I have missed so much in the six months I was gone; well, it was nearly seven with the travel to and from the island.

"Right after you left, and it was Father who was the one to suggest it."

"What court is he from?" Curiosity claws its way out of me.

"Water, Father said we shouldn't marry anyone outside of our court." Hmm. I wonder how he would feel about Lord Killian... maybe he would accept the term since he is a Lord after all.

"Where does your mind wander to, Aisling?" Terreasa asks.

She must have caught me in my own thoughts and I missed an entire conversation.

"Nowhere. Everywhere," I say. Not wanting to give them anything.

"When's the wedding?" I turn to Kourt.

"Two days." She smiles bright.

"Wait, what?" I stutter, surprised by the answer. "Two days? That's so soon..."

"Two days, we wanted you home to celebrate it. Alec couldn't get leave from his outpost, but I wanted to make sure you were home at least," Kourt tells me.

Shocked by how soon the wedding will be, but also my

heart aches with her wanting me home for this, as well as Brother missing out.

The first wedding for all of us, and I thought mine would be first.

"I am so excited for you; I can't wait to help you celebrate your new life!" I beam, I leap out of my chair and give Kourt the biggest hug I can muster.

We have a wedding to plan.

# Chapter Twenty-Two

Two days have passed by so quickly, but that's what happens when you try and plan a wedding in those two days. I didn't think it could be done, but we did it.

I stand in front of my sister, holding back tears of seeing her in her beautiful wedding dress.

"You look beautiful, Kourt," I whisper, keeping the tears from leaking free. I have to be cool, calm, and collected. I'm the one who's holding this family together today.

"Where's Father?" He should have been in here five minutes ago.

"I'll go find him." Turning on my heel, I head for the bedroom door.

"Don't be long! I can do this wedding without him, but I can't without you." Her words strike something deep inside me, I never thought she cared for me so deeply. I choke back a quiet sob and leave the room.

Where could Father be?

I head downstairs to the main living area and don't see him, but I see guests chatting amongst themselves.

"Have you seen Father?" I ask one of them.

We decided to host the wedding at home, the house is... well, it's not really a house but a mini mansion. The yards are quite large to host a wedding, the guests and even tents for those who choose to stay the night. Not many opted for that, but it was an option.

"No, sorry." They shake their heads.

Shit.

I walk into the kitchen and see the maids working hard to get all the meals ready to go after the reception.

"You are all doing amazing, it smells wonderful in here." They smile at me but keep busy.

Could he be in his room? I leave the kitchen and enter the hallway leading to the study and his bedroom. I haven't been in there since Mother passed. I've had no reason to.

I knock on the door and wait for an answer. I don't hear anything, so I spin on my feet and begin to walk away.

"Come in." My father's voice is loud enough to hear. I turn back around; I brace myself with a deep inhale of a breath and turn the door handle.

I step inside his room, expecting it to be dark and dreary but instead it's bright and full of color, exactly the way Mother had it.

He hasn't changed a thing about his room, I get the sudden wave of grief. How sad it would be for him to be in here, day after day.

"The ceremony is about to start." I offer a weak smile.

His first daughter is off to get married... if only he knew that another is counting down the days for her doom.

"Yes, of course, I just needed a minute to gather myself. Thank you for being home." He clears his throat, gathers his suit jacket, and follows me out of his room.

We walk silently back up to Kourt's room and greet the rest of the bridal tribe.

"I'm so glad you're here, Father, I don't think I could do this day without you." She embraces Father and he hugs her back.

"I wouldn't be anywhere else." He pulls her back and wipes a tear away from his eye.

"Let's get married!" I call out to try and break the whatever this atmosphere is right now. Anticipation? Dread? Sorrow? Excitement?

Whatever it is, we need to get the ball rolling.

A few cheers from the ladies carry around the room and the odd feeling has vanished.

The ceremony was gorgeous, Kourt's vows were breathtakingly beautiful. I didn't think she had it in her, but she proved me wrong today. She really must love Grant or find him very attractive to say those words in front of nearly every family member we have and every friend she has. Which is a lot, everyone loves my sister.

We had to invite a few important people from Water Court, since Father was the right-hand man to Lord Marcus.

"How did you find the Academy?" A male voice comes from behind me, I slowly turn to see who it is, and it's Lord Marcus.

Great.

I've never liked the man; he has always given me a bad vibe and sometimes you just have to trust that.

"It was..." How can I put it into words?

"Challenging but rewarding." Two words that I can really summon in this moment of time.

"I was informed that you were one of the top students, that is very impressive." It's like he can't believe those words himself.

"I did my best." I slowly turn to leave but his arm snakes out and grabs my shoulder firmly.

"I also heard about the proposal from Lord Killian." Shivers run up and down my spine. Of course, he knew.

Every Lord in this realm would have heard. I wonder if he has already told my father.

That wouldn't surprise me.

"Yes, well. If I could refuse a Lord, I would have." But unfortunately, that would mean exile or... death.

"A pity, your head would look quite pretty on a spike." He chuckles to himself.

Did I just hear those words from him?

"What did you say?" I turn around, facing him fully. I narrow my eyes at him, showing him I am truly pissed off now.

"Oh, nothing, I just wanted to come over and congratulate you." He clasps his hands behind his back and walks away.

What the actual fuck?


That night, as I'm drifting off to sleep, my mind wanders to Dorian.

I wonder what he is up to and where he is.

*"Dreaming of me?" Dorian's voice is floating all around me, I turn to try and find him, but I don't see him anywhere.*

*"Where are you?" I ask the emptiness of my dream.*

*I'm standing in an empty daisy field. Nothing like I've seen or been in before.*

*"Right behind you." I turn around and see Dorian*

*standing there, arms hanging at either side of his body. Looking glorious in his black armor.*

*"Am I really dreaming this? Or are you really here... in my dream?" I finally ask him. I know he's been in my dreams a few times that seemed so real.*

*"You are smart." He smiles, taking a step toward me.*

*"You can dream walk," I gasp. I've heard of no one having that kind of power.*

*"Does anyone know you can do this?" I ask him. Why would he tell me something so private and classified information?*

*"No. Only you, Sweetheart." He takes another step toward me.*

*"Can you just enter anyone's dream, or do they have to be thinking of you first?" It's a good question, I hope he has to be "invited" in and not enter when he pleases.*

*"It's a complicated answer." He shrugs.*

*"Will you try to answer for me? I truly am curious." This time, I take a step toward him.*

*"At first, I could only enter if someone was having thoughts about me, but as my power grew, so did my ability. I can now enter anyone's mind that I have met before, but as my power grows, I can only assume I can enter anyone's dream with just a thought." That is so fascinating but also scary.*

*"Does distance matter?"*

*"No." He pauses and thinks for a minute. "It's like time and space, it moves different to what we can even put into words, how water flows with the current, how we breathe air, it's just dreams." I have never thought of it like that.*

*"That is an incredible gift." I sigh. I wish I could muster something as extraordinary as that.*

*"So did you come here because I was thinking of you, or*

*did you decide to pop in." It's a question I can't stop myself from asking.*

*"Both. I have missed you." He closes the distance between us.*

*I breathe in his scent, metal and woodsy.*

*Suddenly I feel my body being jerked.*

*No.*

*I don't want to wake up!*

*"Someone is trying to wake me." Panic in my voice, I don't want to leave this place, leave Dorian.*

*"I will visit you again, Sweetheart." He reaches his hand out to stroke my cheek but before I could feel it, my eyes pop wide open and it's my father standing over me.*

"You are going to marry a Lord! And you didn't tell me!" he shouts. Oh, he is really angry.

# Chapter Twenty-Three

My father yelled at me to come down to the living room to discuss my proposal with my sisters. He slammed my door shut, I rubbed at my eyes and sighed. I knew he would find out soon enough, but I was hoping I would be the one to tell him.

My steps to the living room are quiet and cautious. I need to think of what I'm going to say to him.

His voice is loud when I approach the wall joining the living room.

"A Fae Lord, the most powerful in the land! What is she thinking?" The heavy footsteps are pacing back and forth.

"You don't know her side of the story," one of my sisters interjects on my behalf.

"I shouldn't have to listen to her side of the story, she should have declined!!" he retorts back.

"For what? To be exiled or worse... killed?" I step into the room; the vibe is radiating anger and sorrow.

"You could have told me first; we could have worked something out." His tone is softer now, gentler even.

"You weren't at the Academy! You weren't in front of

your entire campus, being chosen to be his bride! How could I tell you; how would you even get there in time? I had no choice but to accept, and I didn't want to tell you because I knew you'd react this way! I had to do what had to be done." I inhale a sharp breath.

I look over at him, pacing the living room. Going back and forth in front of our grand fireplace, there are paintings of us children lining the top of the mantel piece. The dark, rich carpet is being pressed in by his heavy footsteps. The brown and tan clothes cling to him as if he's been sweating from a hard day's work in the garden. No, he's just stressed about this terrible news.

My eyes keep following his every move, wondering how I can get the words out without getting too angry.

"I have no choice but to marry him! You know damn well the rules!" Fury radiates within me.

"You cannot marry the Lord of Fire Court." He doesn't so much as look toward me. Instead, he keeps his head down, like he's ashamed of what's to come.

"How did this happen?" It's very rare for a Fae Lord to seek marriage, usually only those who are fated get married, but maybe Lord Killian hasn't found his yet and is sick of waiting.

My father stops pacing and looks up at me, meeting my eyes for the first time today.

"I will try to talk with Lord Marcus to try and get you out of this, maybe his high position can sway his choice."

I can't believe what he's going to do.

"Why is this such a big deal to you?" I ask him, looking over to my four sisters, sitting in different chairs, hearing what our father is trying to say. They all look too stunned to speak.

All their blond hair is pinned up in tight, neat buns.

Their tight, flowy gowns all in different colors cling to their body, outlining every detail of their curves and muscle under them. They are indeed beautiful. But not one sister turns to look at me. None.

I knew my eldest sister wouldn't have been chosen. Sadly, she lost her mind and leg the night our mother was taken from us. No one ever talks about our mother, but our sister Emmie is the constant reminder of what happened that night. The night Mother was murdered, and my sister was spared her life... what a life that is. I was the only one in the family to care for her.

Kourt, the second eldest, well, she's the one who just got married and is now on her honeymoon.

Then there are my two youngest sisters, Violet and Terreasa. They are both beautiful and youthful.

I wish my brother were here, he makes Father come to his senses. Instead, he's off fighting the ancient war, where I should be, but I'm here. He is my best friend, the only one of my siblings to really care for me. I do truly miss him.

My legs feel shaky from when I stand, sitting still for too long can do that and I march across the living room, but I stop dead in my tracks.

I turn around and point my finger at my father.

"What's done is done. Now you have to decide who takes care of our dear Emmie. Who will tend to her every need? I don't see you bothering to doing it. You never have and I don't think you ever will. Why should Violet and Terreasa do it? They are too young to take on that responsibility! I don't see Kourt doing it! She has her own life now."

"I will take up that responsibility, it shouldn't have been yours to begin with, and I am sorry for not seeing it sooner." He meets my angry gaze and all I see staring back is regret and sorrow. I exhale a breath, my shoulders sag in defeat, and I give a half smile.

"We all miss her too." I turn around for the hallway connecting the entire house, leaving my family in the living room.

This house is like a maze, it's larger than it should be.

The only reason we have this house is because my father was the right-hand man to the Water Lord Marcus but since my mother was murdered, he had to leave that behind. He had to leave all his friends at Court, his passion for working in politics, and alongside his friend Marcus, but Lord Marcus, being so generous to his friend and right-hand man, he decided he wanted to provide for us. So, this house and our lifetime of income is because of him. We are incredibly grateful. Although, we still don't know who murdered my mother, that is another topic for another day.

I walk to my bedroom in silence. Passing the beautiful paintings lining the corridor walls, the blush carpet soft under my feet as I walk away. My bedroom is the only room in the entire house that feels like me, no one can enter and disturb the feel of it.

My room is simple, light-colored walls to match the carpet and curtains. My bed fills the middle of the room, on top of the covers are numerous-sized pillows in array of colors. I have several water paintings lining my walls. I can't paint to save my life so instead I buy them, and water always calms me. Centers me.

Somehow, I knew I was different from my sisters when I was a little girl. I didn't like the typical girly things: the jewels, the dresses, and the fancy balls every Court organizes every other month.

I wanted to stay inside to read my books, get lost in the characters and their exciting lives. That's where I wanted to be... my dream was to visit every library in the world. Although, I'm not sure if it's possible.

Boys... they never piqued my interest. Well, that was until Gerrick at the Academy or Dorian... the boys, the men, they didn't act like they do in books. Charming, devastatingly handsome, and how heroic they are... nope, the opposite sex in the real world is a bit disappointing... but that's okay, I can be my own hero.

I pick up the nearest book to me and flip through the pages, trying to find where I left off. I want to drown out the world, just to forget who I am for just a little while.

Shortly after, there's a knock on the door.

"Come out of you room, Aisling." I hear my father's voice from behind my door. I don't want to face him, don't want to face the reality of my future. I've been trying to come up with solutions on how to avoid my nuptials with Lord Killian. I'm sure he's a great guy, but he's not the guy for me... and I know my fate if I decide to run... it doesn't end pretty.

"Can we please just talk?" I hear the crack in his voice.

I put the book down on my bed and walk toward my bedroom door. I open it and see my father standing there with his head hung down, eyes to the floor, and his hands shaking again in front of him.

"You wanted to talk?" I push open the door and step aside, waiting for him to walk in.

"Yes, I do." He walks in and sits down on my chair in the corner of my room.

"Well, talk."

"I'm sorry about earlier, I shouldn't have yelled at you." He doesn't meet my eyes.

"Who is going to look after Emmie?" I can't bring myself to leave her, I'm the only one who has cared for her.

None of my other sisters know what to do or how to treat Emmie... it's not like after witnessing a murder and nearly dying yourself that you recover easily.

I know I was gone for six months to train, but this is a more permanent situation.

"I will hire someone to look after her." So, he won't do it himself.

"Okay... I guess I can accept that. Why did Lord Killian want me? What do I have to offer him?" I've been asking these questions to myself since the Academy and still come up empty.

"He must know you are kind, selfless, strong, and beautiful. What more can a Lord want in a bride?" He almost smiles.

"I still think this is a mistake..." I sigh.

"When is he coming here?" he asks me. I avoid my father's gaze, not sure if he's ready to hear it.

"Two days."

# Chapter Twenty-Four

Two days... those words echo in my mind.

How can I be someone's bride?

How can I be a Lady of a Court!

My dream was to be stationed with my brother on the front lines after the Academy. This isn't fair.

My mind wanders as the rocks crunch under my feet as I walk along the path through our garden. My eyes soak in all the flowers that are in bloom this spring, I hear the birds chirping away and the buzzing of the bees. It always brings me peace being out here in the sunshine and the fresh air, the rustling of the leaves as the wind slightly picks up. I slide my feet out of my slippers and feel the soft green grass.

I follow the path leading to the borderline of the woods. I never step a toe into the woods, I always stay on the edge. There is something in there that feels off. A gut feeling that danger lies within the border of the woods. I never bothered to ask Father about it.

The path wraps around our entire estate, I continue to follow the path along the woods when I notice a dark figure leaning against a tall oak tree. His entire body is encased in shadows, I can't see any details about him, except that he is tall... very tall.

I pause, do I dare approach him?

Yes. I inhale a deep breath and stalk toward this figure.

"Sweetheart, should you be here?" he says when I'm a few feet away. His voice is rich and masculine but familiar.

"No." I tilt my chin up higher, showing no fear.

But there is fear... plenty of it.

Who is this man? Why does it seem like I already know him?

"Then why are you here?" He doesn't move a muscle.

"I could ask you the same thing." I take a step closer, but he growls.

"The woods aren't safe, go back home." He takes a step back, away from me.

I take his advice, bend down and quickly slide my slippers back on, and turn around, leaving him still leaning against the tree.

What just happened?

Why did he seem so familiar?

I quickly hurry along the path back to the house, needing to get back inside and collect my thoughts.

Why was he in the woods?

"Is that you, Aisling?" my father calls from the living room. I close the back door behind me.

"Yes, it's me."

"Can you come in here, please? There is someone here who wants to see you." I don't know if I can handle talking to someone politely right now.

I drag my feet to the living room and spot a man standing with his back to me. He has his left hand resting against the mantelpiece above the fireplace.

"Lord Marcus has stopped by," my father announces our Water Lord.

Shit.

Another run-in with the Lord himself.

Lord Marcus turns around and his blue-gray eyes glint with trouble. I have this sick feeling in my gut whenever he comes to visit.

His pale white hair in curls around his pointy ears and royal blue uniform always looking fresh. He stands straighter when looking at me. Like I hold the truth, whatever that truth is.

"Welcome to our home, Lord Marcus," I say with a low curtsy.

"The pleasure is mine, Aisling. I'm sorry I couldn't stop the process for your hand in marriage to Lord Killian." He acts like our conversation at my sister wedding never existed.

"It's fine," is all I can say.

"What's your agenda for today's visit?" my father asks him.

"I wanted to check in on Aisling before she leaves and offer my services to you."

"Oh?" I shouldn't be so surprised. Lord Marcus and my father are close friends.

"Yes, I want to give you a little gift." He walks toward me and hands me a small black box.

I open it and inside is a small, round, blue glass ball. Confusion must show on my face.

"It's an orb. A magical orb. When you are living in Fire Court and wish to see your family, just ask it. If you wish to leave Fire Court without alarming anyone, it'll vanish you to wherever you'd like to go." I never knew such magical items existed. Of course, everyone who is Fae has their own elemental powers, but we don't use them unless we must.

"This one is from my personal collection, only Lords of courts have such items... so maybe you'll have something of your own once you become Lady Aisling." I meet Lord Marcus's eyes, there's a hint of danger, a daring in them.

"Thank you, this is very thoughtful!" I politely smile.

Lord Marcus turns to my father.

"I know Aisling will be leaving soon, and I know she was taking care of poor Emmie before the Academy, so I thought you'd like some help with her." Lord Marcus gives a swift movement with his hands and in a burst of water, a bubble appears and there steps out a woman. She's short, black hair cut into a pixie haircut and she's wearing white and brown servant clothes. Why would he summon her here?

"Meet Anama." Lord Marcus gestures to the woman.

"She is here to help with poor Emmie, and whatever else you might get her to do around here." A wicked smile spreads across his lips.

"Welcome to our home, Anama," my father greets her.

In acceptance, she just nods at my father.

"I'll show you to your room and you can meet Emmie." I do a low curtsy to Lord Marcus and turn around to head for the hallway leading to the grand staircase.

It's silent on the walk to one of the spare bedrooms on the second floor of our home.

"This one can be your room, please let my father know if you'd like to change anything within here. It will be no problem, please make this your home." I open the door to her room and it's simple. A large bed against the farthest wall in the room, the two large windows let enough light in, and a writing desk opposite the bed in the other corner.

"Thank you," she says quietly.

"Come on, let's go meet Emmie." I turn around to continue down the hallway we just came and back down the stairs.

"Emmie's bedroom is on the bottom floor; she can't get up and down the stairs so we made her comfortable in the old study," I say to Anama.

My father had no use for this room anymore, not since he stopped working for Lord Marcus.

I knock on Emmie's door three times, letting her know we are about to enter.

"Emmie doesn't talk but can motion her needs. Food, drink, move, and toilet. I can teach you them and you'll need to assist her to dress, shower, and move spots within the house. It's full-on but so rewarding spending time with her. She does have her personality; you just need to know what to look out for."

Emmie is sitting in her usual chair by the window, that overlooks the beautiful gardens. I think it's her favorite place, it was before her tragic accident.

"Hey, Emmie, I have someone here for you to meet." I gesture for Anama to step forward in front of Emmie.

Emmie looks at her, takes her in, and raises her eyebrows. I knew she would react like that.

"This is Anama, she is going to take of you while I'm away at Fire Court." I know she was there when my father told me the news, but I'm not sure how much she actually took in, so this is my way of reminding her that I am going to be leaving soon.

"It's lovely to meet you." Anama takes a seat opposite her. I watch the two together; I think this will be a great fit.

I slowly back away, listening to Anama tell Emmie about her family and her interests.

This is going to be okay.

I know I can always look into the orb and check up on Emmie while I'm away.

Two days...

That's all I've got left of my old life.

# Chapter Twenty-Five

It's been two long days and now today is the day my entire life will change.

"Aisling, can you come downstairs, please?" I hear my father's call from downstairs.

I'm not ready to face my new future.

I grab my heavily packed backpack from the bed and head for the bedroom door, before closing it I stop and take in one last glimpse of my room. This could be the last time I'm ever in here.

A bittersweet moment.

I take the steps slowly, not ready to meet my fate.

I hear quiet voices coming from the living room.

"Lord Killian, it's a pleasure to have you in our house." My father, always polite.

"Pleasure's mine, I am here to collect my bride." His deep voice rings in my ears.

*His bride...*

My feet reach the bottom of the stairs, hesitant to see Lord Killian again.

My lungs fill with air as I round the corner to where I

meet my father and Lord Killian.

"Ah, there she is." My father beams. Of course, he is excited for me to go, it's not like he wanted me home anyway.

There, standing in the middle of the room is a tall man. Possibly six foot four, wearing a black suit, matching his jet-black hair cut short, back and sides. He turns around at the sound of my feet on the carpet.

His eyes drinking me in, he starts from my shoes to the top of my head. I feel self-conscious with the dress I chose to wear. The pale blue, matching my eyes, and my hair in braids, pinned up on top of my head.

"Stunning," I hear him quietly murmur.

I shiver at the sound.

There is something powerful that surrounds him, maybe it's the way he carries himself or knowing he is the most powerful Lord in the realm.

And I am to be his bride.

"Are you ready to go home, Aisling?" he asks me while he holds out his right hand for me to take.

I look around the room and not one of my sisters is present, not to see me go, only my father.

I take Lord Killian's outstretched hand and walk out the front door, leaving my old life behind, ready for my new one.

* * *

"I have to make a stop in Air Court, I have a meeting with Lord Tatum about some business of mine." We are sitting in a carriage, face-to-face. Not much room in here to make space between us.

"I've never been to Air Court before, is it as lovely as

they say?" I watch Lord Killian's mouth twitch a little into a small smile.

"It is, but I do have to say my... our home is the most beautiful in Archurillia."

"Oh, I'm sure it is lovely." I smile shyly.

"How long of a trip is it to Air Court?"

"About two days, we will stop in a tavern before it gets dark," Lord Killian answers.

It goes quiet and I look out the carriage window, looking at the tall trees passing by, people walking by foot alongside the road with bags and meat thrown across their shoulders, the women walking with their babies in their arms, and I am in here with a Lord.

I shouldn't be here, I should be using my training skills to fight, to do something that truly matters. Instead, I'm sitting here in a carriage with a Lord who wants to make me his trophy wife. How is this fair?

"A zillard for your thoughts?" Money, if only he'd dare pay me...

"Just wondering why, I was chosen from the Academy. There were plenty of choices there, why choose someone from there to begin with? I have sisters who would be better suited for the role. I will also miss my family, even though I was already gone six months, to not know if I will ever return scares me..." I admit out loud.

"I never realized you have such a large family."

"I do, there is also my brother, who is off fighting the war against the humans, who I hardly see, and I thought I was going to reunite with him..." Now, I don't think I will see him for a long time.

"Ah, the war... yes, most of my and Earth Court's troops are fighting in it." There is a hint of sadness in his tone.

"I know the difficult feeling it is having a loved one in

war... my half brother, Dorian, is leading my men." Dorian? Surely it can't be... *my*... Dorian? Maybe I can try and find out. It's odd finding out personal information about a Lord, knowing he has a half brother, but then again, I don't know much about this Fire Lord.

"Are you two close?" I pry.

"Not really, we were brought up differently, so it was hard to form that sibling bond." Again, a hint of sadness in his tone.

"That sounds like a lonely childhood, I'm sorry." I place my hand on top of his. Hoping the small gesture gives him some comfort.

The carriage comes to a sudden halt. I look to Lord Killian for answers, and he just opens the door and steps out.

He turns back at me and says, "Wait here." He closes the door behind him.

I can hear low voices talking amongst themselves. I wonder what could be happening out there.

"You can come out now, Aisling," Lord Killian calls out to me.

I inhale a deep breath before opening the carriage door and stepping out into the fresh air.

I let out a deep groan as I stretch out my legs.

It was maybe two or three hours already in our journey to Air Court.

"You have to fix it!" Lord Killian's temper is rising.

"I'm sorry, My Lord, but we do not have the right tools with us. You will have to either take the horse or continue by foot," the driver of the carriage replies.

Lord Killian runs his left hand through his hair in frustration. It's nice to see a Lord be so normal.

He turns to me. "How are you with horses?"

"Terrible." I nervously laugh.

"All right." He turns to the driver. "You will take the horse to go to the nearest town to get the tools you'll need. Come back here and fix it." The man nods.

"We will continue by foot, once the carriage is fixed, drop our belongings off at Herphoin Tavern." The man nods once more, and he climbs onto the saddle of the brown horse.

"Have you been in the woods before?" Another question from Lord Killian.

"Ah... no. I haven't really walked into the woods. I've always stayed within our boundaries." I watch as he gathers supplies from the carriage.

"It's going to get cold tonight, so put this cloak on." He hands me a black cloak with the fire symbol embroidered on the back.

It hits me... I now belong to Fire Court... to him.

"There's only a two-hour walk from here to Herphoin." My stomach grumbles, knowing there is a two-hour wait before we can eat.

"I'll feed and bathe you soon." Lord Killian picks up the last of the supplies, I turn away to hide the heat in my cheeks. Bathe? Oh no...

"Lord Killian, why did you choose me?" We start to walk alongside the road, just like I saw the men and women earlier. I wonder if they do this daily, would they get tired and have to camp in the woods?

"Please, call me Killian. You don't need to say my title... not when you're to be my bride." I look over to him, walking too close to me that our shoulders occasionally brush together.

"I was drawn to you. Your scoring was one of the highest in the Academy, so it was a no-brainer." That really

doesn't explain why. I will get down to the bottom of why...
one day.


The next two hours are long and quiet except for the
occasional small talk, but we finally make it to Herphoin
Tavern.

"Finally," I breathe.

"Let's get food into your belly before a nice soak... shall
we?" He holds out his hand again for me to take. The feel of
his soft hand somehow gives me comfort.

"Lord Killian, we are so glad to have you stay with us,"
the woman behind the bar greets him.

"We will have whatever you're serving tonight." Killian
tosses a coin pouch on the countertop. The woman scoops it
up fast and starts shouting orders.

"Let's head up to our room, away from prying eyes and
ears." He leads us to the stairs in the corner.

The room isn't as small as I thought it would be, but
having two people in here does make it seem confining.

He walks to the fireplace first and with a flick of his
wrist, the wood bursts with red and orange flame. Instantly
this little room starts to warm up.

"I'll run the bath now." Killian moves to the little tub at
the other end of the room and turns a tap. "Mmm, cold," he
says to himself. With a touch of his finger, I see a tiny red
flame seep out of his index finger and lick the water.

We all have powers being Fae, but I'm always in awe
when I see other elemental Faes using theirs. Even at the
Academy, it was a magical time. Seeing other students use
their magic, harness it, and use it. I think that was my
favorite part.

"Thank you," I say quietly in the space between us.

# Chapter Twenty-Six

"Undress and get in the bath, Aisling," Killian orders me. I am absolutely freezing so it doesn't take much for me to strip off my dress, let down my hair, and step over the side of the bath.

The warm water softly touches my legs and I slowly sink down.

I let out a little moan of pleasure.

Heaven.

Killian is being a gentleman and turns around while I undress, it bothers me for a split second but after the water hits, I don't care who sees me naked.

"May I wash you?" Killian turns around but doesn't take a step closer to the bath.

"No." I blush at the directness, I know I shouldn't say no, he is to be my husband, My Lord after all. I just want a sense of privacy, for a bath at least.

Killian nods, turns toward the door, and exhales.

"I'll be downstairs if you need me." He opens the bedroom door and leaves me soaking in the bath.

I know I should have let him wash me, but I think it's too soon. Not when my thoughts are still on Dorian.

* * *

I didn't hear him come back in the room last night and when I woke this morning, he wasn't in the room either.

"I've brought you breakfast." He places a small plate with bread and fruit on the side table next to the bed.

"Thank you," I murmur.

It feels a little awkward between us.

I can't put my finger on it but I see him a little differently.

He's supposed to be the most powerful Lord in the realm but being with him here, he's soft and charming. He doesn't seem that powerful to me.

Maybe everyone has it wrong.

"Are you ready to go?" Killian is leaning against the doorframe.

"Yes, I'm ready to go to Air Court. I can't wait to meet Lord Tatum."

"You'll find he's more charming than me, so watch out..." He winks.

"I doubt anyone can be more charming than you." I smile when I walk past him.

"Oh, you have no idea." He chuckles behind me.

I think he can sense the awkwardness between us, maybe he is trying to get us out of this spot.

Outside the tavern, there is our carriage waiting.

"It's fixed?" I look to the brand-new wheel mounted on the carriage.

Of course, it was, with his type of money and reputation I knew it wouldn't take long.

"Yes, now let's get back onto the road if we want to make it to Air Court before dark." He takes my hand in his and we walk to the carriage door.

It's already open, Killian helps me up the two steps and I sit inside the small space again. This time, I'm not worried if I brush my leg against his, or if I catch him looking at me.

Halfway through the trip, he turns and looks at me.

"Did you sleep well?"

"I did, thank you; I didn't hear you come in the room last night." I wonder where he slept, if he did... maybe the floor?

"I got another room; I didn't want to impose on you while you slept." Killian winks at me.

"What kind of business do you have with Lord Tatum?" I'm not sure why I even ask, he probably won't tell me.

"I just need to discuss Court matters, nothing to worry you about." Vague. I get it. None of my business.

"Will I be allowed to be present for the meeting?" I know I am pushing it.

"No. You can take a tour around Air Court, get to sight-see." Of course.

I look out the window, trying to calm myself. How can I be his Lady if he won't let me in on his Court business? Don't I have the right to know?

"There are many places to visit within Air Court, I heard the library is a wonderful starting place, as well as the Fountain of Airises." I don't know why he bothers. I'm not interested in this conversation anymore. The quicker we get to Air Court, the better.

# Chapter Twenty-Seven

Air Court is so beautiful, I can't believe my eyes. The way the palace looks, it's like something out of a painting. The way the light green vines decorate the white brick walls, the beautiful clear blue sky, there is no cloud in sight. The air is still, no trace of wind but it's not too hot nor too cold. It's like magic, making it the perfect temperature.

"Wow, this is amazing." I exhale a deep breath; I had no idea I was holding.

"See, now you can go sightsee. I won't be long and then if you'd like we can stay a night before heading back onto the road to home." The way he says *home* has so much emotion to it. Our home.

"Thank you, Killian. Truly." I look up into his eyes, I see a hint of admiration toward me. I feel my cheeks heat up at the intense look.

"Let me get someone to accompany you, I know there is certain history here that I'm sure would intrigue you." He takes my hand, and we walk past the golden front gates of the palace.

There in front of us is the grand staircase.

It's pure white, it's like walking on a cloud.

"It's a pleasure to see you again, Killian." A male voice floats from the top of the stairs.

I look up and see a very beautiful male. The first thing I notice about him is his pure white hair, short but styled in wisps. He takes the steps toward us. His clothes are also white, but with blue lining. He must be Lord Tatum, of Air Court.

"Pleasure is always mine, Tatum." I watch as Killian next to me bows his head to him. I've never seen a Lord bow to another Lord. I thought they hold their own... fascinating.

A closer inspection, I see Lord Tatum has the palest blue eyes I've ever seen, but I'm not surprised. His skin is tanned, probably from being out in the sun every day. He is beautiful.

"Who do we have here? This is a first for you to bring a guest." Lord Tatum turns to me, looking me up and down,with curiosity in his eyes.

"This is my bride-to-be, Aisling." I copy Killian, but this time I curtsy, bending down low.

"Pleasure to meet you, Aisling, what an honor to meet the wife-to-be of Killian." He takes my free hand and brings it up to his mouth. He slowly kisses the back of my hand.

I look toward Killian to get his reaction, but his face gives nothing away.

"Lord Tatum, your home is magnificent," I say when he releases my hand.

"Call me Tatum, or Tate. I don't like the formal titles amongst friends." He smiles. What is it with these Lords and not wanting to be formal? I like it, but it's something I'm so surprised about.

"Is there anyone who could show Aisling around while

we have our meeting?" Killian looks around the entrance, there isn't a soul insight.

"Of course, I can get my wife, Lady Trish." As if he breathed a certain way, someone appears out of thin air.

"Wonderful!" Killian says with delight, he leans down to whisper in my ear while Tate talks with a servant.

"Keep your answers short with Lady Trish, she can get bored very quickly and you don't want to piss her off. I like having Tate as my friend." Killian brushes his lips against the base of my ear.

I just nod. I don't have the words to speak.

I'm not sure how I feel about this type of chemistry with him, the closeness.

Why couldn't a servant show me around? At least then I would know the ins and outs of this palace, instead of the places where I should be shown around, but how can I deny the Lord and Lady of Air?

"Let's go to the briefing room, Lady Trish will meet us there." Lord Tatum starts to lead us to the right; it doesn't look like we are taking the stairs. That must be where the bedrooms are.

The little hallway we walk down is covered in the same green vines along the walls, and it leads us through a dark tunnel.

I clutch Killian's hand tighter. I don't know what to expect.

I shouldn't be this afraid, I've faced worse at the Academy.

He rubs his thumb over my hand, giving me a silent reassurance.

I can see the light at the end of the tunnel, once we reach the entrance there is pure brightness.

I blink a few times to clear the darkness from them.

The room before me has a large round table, it looks like it can seat twenty people.

"This is amazing," I breathe. I try to keep my voice low; I am just in awe.

"Thank you, Aisling, I take pride in making each room in my palace a place where everyone can enjoy. No matter the means of it." He takes a seat at the head of the table.

"Are you sure I can't stay?" I turn to Killian, pleading with my eyes.

I don't want to be feeling this small in an unknown place.

"No, I'm sorry. Maybe next time?" I already know there won't be a next time, he'll probably come without me or again won't include me.

"Sure." I tug my hand out of his, and that's when I hear a faint laughter. A laughter that makes my skin crawl. That better not be Lady Trish.

The laughter gets louder and louder.

"Ah, my beautiful wife is here." Tatum gets up from his seat and greets his wife at the entrance we just came out of.

Shit.

How can I be around someone who I can't tolerate?

I know that's mean to say but seriously.

It's the laugh.

Maybe I could try and not make her laugh when we take a tour around the palace, yes, that's the plan.

"Please greet our guests, I'm sure you remember Lord Killian, and his bride-to-be... Aisling." My eyes scan Lady Trish's figure. She takes us in and bows her head to Killian.

She's wearing a flowy blue gown, bright gold jewelry, and her stunning red hair floats down in curls wrapped around her back.

She is beautiful.

"It's a pleasure to see you again, Lord Killian, although it has been too long since you visited me." Her smile is sweet, but I can hint jealousy in her eyes when she finally takes me in.

"Aisling, what an unusual name. What does it mean?" It's not unusual... I frown at her straightforwardness.

"It means dream, a vision," Killian jumps in, rescuing me. A small smile forming at my lips, I avert my eyes to the ground.

My hero.

"Very well," she murmurs to herself.

"Back to business, Tate?" Killian asks Tatum, trying to break the awkwardness that's creeped into the room.

"Yes, of course. Wife, why don't you take Aisling, the visitor, on a tour of the palace. Take her to all your favorite spots." Tatum blows a kiss to his wife when she nods her head in obedience.

"Are you sure I can't stay?" I plead harder with my eyes.

"No, go enjoy yourself. Just watch your tongue... or I will find other means for it later." He smirks at me. The heat in my cheeks returns.

"Fine." I bow my head to both the Lords and follow Lady Trish out of the large meeting room.

* * *

"How was your tour?" Killian and I have returned to our room, we decided to stay the night and continue to Fire Court tomorrow.

"It was pleasant."

"Just pleasant? I'm surprised you didn't leave her and explore on your own."

"Well, I wouldn't be the greatest guest, now, would I?" I

fluff the right-side pillow. I am exhausted but grateful for a comfortable bed tonight.

It definitely looks better than the tavern bed.

"How was your meeting? Did you get everything sorted that you need?" I lie down on top of the bed. I'm exhausted but my body is still on high alert, being in a place I'm not used to.

"I did, although we kept getting sidetracked by going down memory lane, Lord Tatum is known for that. Always trying to change the subject from the important task at hand." Killian shakes his head and laughs.

"I'll find another room to stay in, I don't want to impose on your space." Killian looks around the room awkwardly.

"Would you mind staying?" I really don't want to be alone in this place.

"I can sleep on the couch." He starts walking toward the couch, I know I should offer him the bed since this is his friend's court, but I don't have it in me.

"Thank you." I say sleepily, feeling myself drift off to slumber.

# Chapter Twenty-Eight

"We have reached the border of Fire Court, your new home." Killian reaches over and picks up my hand, and gives it a squeeze before letting go.

I wonder what he will be like in his own environment, surrounded by his own people.

"Is it hot there?" A silly question I'm sure, as Water Court isn't cold as you'd expect, nor is Air Court.

"No, although, I do have the magic to change the temperature to your liking." That is amazing. Only a Lord can do such magic.

"I'm sure it will be fine." I look out the window at the passing trees, they are the same you see throughout Archirillia.

There are butterflies starting to form in the pit of my stomach as we near the formal gates of Fire Court.

"Welcome home, Aisling." Killian smiles at me as we pass the dark black gates that are so high my neck cracks from looking up. We take the path leading to the front door of the palace. It's not how I expected Killian's palace to look, it's nothing like Air Court's palace. The tall walls of the palace are a slighter shade black to the gates out front, there are deep red roses planted in garden beds along the stairs to the front doors. The stairs are painted pure white, making the area brighter than it needs to be.

"We are home." Killian exits the carriage and offers his hand to me; I take it and step out of the carriage after him.

"It's beautiful," I murmur.

"You haven't seen my favorite part." He smiles fondly at his home.

"Will you show me?"

"I will show you every inch of my home, Ash. I want you to love it as much as I." Killian and I take the white steps together in silence.

The ceilings are extremely high, the walls are pure white and there are black lines lining the middle of the walls, wrapping around the entire room. The black marble tiles sparkle under my feet.

"This room is beautiful," I murmur.

"This is nothing, come... I'll show you my favorite place." Killian grabs my hand and leads me down a corridor to the left of the palace, no idea where he is leading me. I take in the corridor lined with large windows on the left side and paintings lined on the right wall, there are large plant pots along the wall, in the pots are the same deep red roses. They are beautiful.

"Are roses your favorite?" I ask Killian when we walk through another corridor that connects with the last, this time there are no windows but still had paintings and potted roses.

"No, they were my mother's. I never had the heart to change them."

"That is lovely, she sounds wonderful."

"She was..." His voice goes quiet.

We round the corner and suddenly stop short.

"What?" I mutter out.

"Brother..." A deep male voice echoes from down the corridor, it feels familiar, but I can't quiet put my finger on it.

"Ah, you are to meet my half brother, Dorian. He shouldn't be home for another four weeks." I feel Killian tense next to me, it tells me he isn't that fond of his sibling.

"Dorian," Killian answers his brother.

Dorian walks with pace to greet us, his entire being radiates confidence and cockiness.

"You're home early, I thought the rotation shouldn't be happening for another four weeks." The war, Killian vaguely mentioned he likes to try and rotate his men so they can be home with their families, as the war isn't a threat to worry about right now. Of course, that will all change if there's a shift in the war.

I wish Water Court did this, then we would get a chance to have my brother home once in a while. Now with being locked up here, I won't get the chance to reunite with him.

"The men decided I should come home to greet you; it was their idea. You can take it up with your second-in-command."

"Fine," Killian grumbles under his breath.

"Who do we have here?" Dorian shifts his attention to me, like he's never laid eyes on me before, not like we have shared moments together, dreams even. Is this his way of keeping our knowing each other a secret? If so, I can play along too.

"This is Aisling, my wife-to-be." This is when Killian

straightens, like he is being protective of me. I find that...
concerning.

"Aisling..." he says with confidence, "Sweetheart." He
barely breathes the word but I heard it.

Oh, Dorian... why did you have to be a half brother with
the man I'm to marry?

My breath hitches in my throat, my pulse begins to
pound in my veins. That word.

The realization on my face must show as Dorian smirks
at me.

I try to quickly hide it so I'm not asked by Killian what
is going on. I must find time alone with Dorian. I need to
ask him questions... so many questions.

What was so dangerous about them?

"Dorian." I bow my head to him, after all he is the
Lord's brother.

My soon-to-be family.

That thought makes me sick to my stomach.

Dorian reaches up with his hand and brushes his fingers
through his hair. His hair is the same jet-black as Killian's,
but Dorian's hair is curly and the length is just past his
pointed ears, long enough he could put it in a bun. His eyes
are similar to Killian's but they have a hint of purple aura.
There's something about them that feels like my own.

"Shall we continue?" Killian brings me back to the
present.

"Yes, please." I take his outstretched arm and tuck my
hand around his as he leads me away from Dorian.

I quickly glance behind me to find Dorian still standing
there, watching us walk away.

"Sorry about my brother, he can be awkward at first."

"I didn't know you had a brother; no one talks about
family members of the Lords." I wonder why that is.

"He's my half brother, he prefers to be kept out of the family tree and our parents agreed, although, our mother... who we share, would disagree." I hear a faint sadness in his tone, I wonder how long it has been since he saw her.

"What happened to your parents?"

"They both died, that's how I became Lord. A fire when Dorian and I were just boys." How awful, especially with it being a fire.

I can't possibly imagine losing both my parents to such a fate, I am grateful I've still got my father, even though he isn't much of a father to me and my siblings.

"She would have loved you, Aisling." I look up at Killian and my smile matches his. That's lovely to say.

"Come on, I still have to show you my favorite spot." I know he's trying to make the mood light again.

At the end of this corridor there is a dark brown wooden door.

Killian opens the door and inside is a narrow staircase, leading up, we take the deep red steps, slowly making our way to the top. It's so cold, the hairs on my arms stand. The air whispers sweet nothings and the space is small, only allowing one person to take the steps up at a time.

Once we reach the top, Killian turns to me. "Close your eyes."

So, I do.

I feel the door open when warmth greets my skin, scaring away the cold.

"This is my favorite place, ever since I was a boy. No one is allowed up here. If you need a place to just think, please come here." The words hold such passion, this must be a magical place.

"Open your eyes, Ash," Killian whispers into my ear.

I do.

My breath is taken away, the sight in front of me is magical, indeed.

There, in the near distance is the largest volcano I've ever seen. The lava dances on top of the mountain but never spills down.

"It's beautiful," I tell Killian.

"Beautiful, indeed..." I turn to see Killian looking at me instead of the mountain. My cheeks turn red from the heat.

This man knows how to continue to make me blush.

# Chapter Twenty-Nine

"**D**inner will be ready in an hour," Killian tells me while he's leading me to our bedroom. I don't think I will get over the whole *our* phrase.

"You can freshen up before we head back downstairs, I know I want to shower the journey off me." At the end of the hallway, I spot a large black door covered in swirls of flames. I can only guess that this is our bedroom.

"Are you sure you don't want me to stay somewhere else?" I'm not sure I'm ready to share a room with Killian yet.

"You are to be my bride; we must have a united front for the Court." He sighs and pushes open the double doors, and my breath immediately hitches.

The room is nothing like I've seen before, it's as large as our entire second floor back at my father's house.

"Do you really need this much space?" I turn to Killian, trying to mask my surprise.

"Well, I did get lonely, but now I get to share it with you." Of course, the entire room isn't just for his bed, on the right side there is the built-in wardrobe, and I can see both sides are full of clothes. I step toward it, curious to see his clothes, what he would wear, and how he stores them.

I'm surprised to see long, flowing dresses, gowns, silk pajamas and undergarments. *My clothes.*

"These aren't my clothes," I say out loud.

"No, but I had the lady's maids go shopping for you, per my request."

"They are lovely." I've never had anything more exquisite in my life.

I see his clothes neatly lined up. Mostly suits but I can see some casual clothes, track pants, shirts, and jeans. I wonder when he gets the chance to wear them.

"I'm going to shower in another room, you can have this one." Killian leads us both past the large bed in the middle of the room, and I mean *large* bed. I've never seen anything that big before. It's a four-poster bed, with white curtains wrapped around it, giving privacy to us if anyone happens to enter the room.

I wish that wasn't the case, but I have to keep remembering that I'm to be his bride.

The bathroom has no doors, but it's as large as the built-in wardrobe. The shower is three times the size of a regular one, there is even a sitting bench in there. I wonder what type of activities we could get up to on there.

'Bath or shower?" he asks. I think about it for a moment.

"Shower..." I say.

Killian walks to the shower door, opens it, and steps in. He turns the two taps and waits for the water to warm up.

"No magic?" I ask.

"No need, you live in Fire Court now." I should have known that everything is powered by the volcano and the magic that runs through the land and in my Lord.

"The water is set to the perfect temperature." Killian steps out of the shower.

"Thank you." I watch as he turns to leave the bathroom and closes the door behind him.

Now I'm left to my own thoughts in silence.

* * *

The grand dining room is breathtaking. I've never seen such a large dining table before. It could seat at least twenty people comfortably and still seat extra if needed.

I sit at one end of the table while I wait for Killian to arrive. I'm sure he will sit next to me, so we can talk about the events that are to follow, now that I'm here.

"Is this seat taken... sweetheart?" A male voice comes from behind me, my neck stretches to look back and I see Dorian.

My skin crawls with electricity, my magic within my blood hums.

"Ah... I didn't know you were joining us for dinner." I finally get the words out.

"Well, I do live here, and it would be rude to miss dinner with my brother and his... future bride" His last words sound like venom on his tongue.

"Have you seen Killian?" I ask.

"No, I thought he was with you." Dorian looks at the outstretched table and decides to sit next to me. The closest chair, no space between us.

The hum of my disapproval is loud enough for him to turn to me and raise his eyebrow.

"You don't want me sitting here? I thought you'd be thrilled with me being so close to you." I can hear the sarcasm.

"No, I don't." That is a lie, but I have to keep up this facade.

"Why don't you move to the middle of the table, or closer to Killian? I'm sure he'd be excited to talk to you..." My attention shifts when the waiters start bringing out the food for us to eat. Everything smells divine.

Dorian makes no attempt to move.

Great.

"Sorry I'm late, I had an urgent matter to take care of. Hello, Brother. I wasn't sure you'd be joining us tonight." Killian takes a seat opposite me at the table.

That leaves Dorian too close, and no buffer.

"I wasn't at first, but then I decided to make an appearance. I'm excited to get to know Aisling, where she grew up, her favorite flowers, and her thoughts on being sold like a piece of meat." My breath hitches. Is he trying to start a fight with Killian?

"As much as I like when you play house with what belongs to me, Dorian, I will not tolerate this behavior in front of my wife-to-be." Killian stands and slams his fist on the top of the dining table. I'm not sure I like this kind of anger.

I guess the Fire Lord must have a hot head.

"Forgive me, Aisling. As beautiful as you are, I rather like my head." Dorian stands from his seat, reaches over, grabs my hand, places a soft kiss, and winks at me before exiting the dining hall.

The heat in my cheeks returns... I have to try to mask it away. Killian can't catch on that we know each other.

"I am sorry about my brother. He doesn't know boundaries with what's mine and his... one day it will get him into trouble," Killian apologizes.

I turn my attention back to the food in front of me. The

awkwardness between us floats around the room. Why did Dorian have to make comments like that?

"Do you have any plans for tomorrow?" I ask Killian when he's shoving food quickly into his mouth. Is he trying to hurry so he can leave?

"Yes."

That is the only answer I get. I continue eating my food, not sure what else I can say to lighten the mood. It's completely awkward.

I've never wanted a night to end so quickly in my life.

# Chapter Thirty

## Killian

"I want to host a ball here in Fire Court, to celebrate you becoming my wife." I roll over to my side and admire how beautiful Aisling looks.

I wonder when she will get used to the idea that she will become my wife. I hate sleeping in another room away from her.

"It's just, I don't want to make a big deal about it. Becoming your wife, this should be something between you and me." She's deep in thought, I can tell by how she crunches her nose a little.

I've been studying her facial expressions; I want to know everything there is to know about her... although, I did notice her body language around Dorian. I have to ask her about that, maybe tread lightly about the topic. I don't want her to pull away from me.

"Unfortunately, Ash, you are to become a *Lady*. You will have to learn to rule the Fire Court alongside me and that puts you in the public eye. Balls, festivals, weddings, important announcements are a part of your job now." I try to make her aware that she will be a public figure.

"What about meetings about important stuff? Will I be included in that?" She huffs when she gets off the bed and I watch her go back and forth, pacing in our bedroom. Her cute nightgown flows in the opposite direction she's walking in.

"No. They are only for me; we don't allow women in meetings to discuss our courts." I wish she would learn the customs of how a Lord and Lady conduct themselves. Maybe I could ask Gerald to give her some lessons before the ball. That should ease things around here.

Gerald has been my best friend since I can remember, he is the brother I wish Dorian would be like, but instead I got Gerald as a friend. I'm more than happy with that, we get along so well and he's always there when I need him.

"I'll introduce you to Gerald later, I'm sure you'll enjoy his company." I get up from the bed, ending this discussion.

* * *

"I was wondering when I would get the chance to meet your future wife!" Gerald punches me in the arm. It's so good to see him, it's only been three weeks. He is my right-hand man and has a responsibility to go to other courts to sort out the lesser business for me. He was born an Earth Fae, but he moved to Fire Court when his mother was exiled. I still don't know why, and I'm too nervous to ask him.

"It's a pleasure to meet you, Gerald." Aisling does a small curtsy.

I am showing Aisling my library and art collection when Gerald proudly walks in. I thought he would have arrived a little later from his letter last night.

"The pleasure is all mine, beautiful." I watch these two interact with one another, I see the blush creep into her cheeks. Gerald has always been a player, but my women were always off-limits... or so I thought.

I hold my hand out for Ash to take and she looks between Gerald and myself. For a split second she hesitates but takes my hand anyway. Phew.

"Tell me about yourself, Aisling," Gerald asks Ash when I lead us all out of the library and toward the gardens of the palace. I've made sure I've set a quiet brunch for us.

"There isn't much to know, really." She tucks her hair behind her left ear. A nervous trait?

"Come on, there must be some kind of gossip you could tell us," Gerald adds.

"Well... I am one of six children. I adore my brother, who's my best friend, and I miss him dearly. Although I wish I was reunited with him on the front lines." The sadness in her tone makes my heart ache.

"The war?" Gerald asks.

"Yes." She is lost in thought; I'll try to distract her.

"I met Aisling at the Academy, that's how I chose her to be my bride. Her father seems like a nice man from our interaction... but maybe that was just him being a subject." I shrug my shoulders.

"Ha, yes. My mother was murdered, and my sister was so traumatized by the event she lost her mind... and leg," she says with more anger in her tone. I never knew that; I should have done my research before asking Ash to be my bride. That kind of baggage can do damage to my public image.

Shit.

I also noticed she didn't mention the Academy, why would she try to keep that to herself?

"Have they caught the person?" I ask, once we reach the

small round white table in the middle of the lush green lawn.

Surrounding us are hidden servants in amber clothing in the large bushes. Only I can see them, the perks of being glammed.

"No, but becoming Killian's bride I will take advantage of my status and form an investigation. I want closure for my family. I need it." She looks down at her shaky hands.

I reach out and hold them in my own. I never knew this. I'm not sure what help I can give.

"I'll help you," Gerald says, more cheerful than he needs to be.

"Oh, thank you, Gerald, that would mean so much to me." She pulls her hands from mine and leans across the table to kiss him on the cheek. I shouldn't be jealous, but my blood is boiling at the act.

"You're welcome. Did you want to start straightaway, or would you rather wait for your new title?" *Very noble, Gerald,* I seethe silently.

I look over to the servants hiding and nod my head, giving them the all clear to start bringing out the food. I need the distraction.

"Straightaway," Ash looks over toward me, meeting my eye contact. "Is that okay?" She's asking for my permission; how can I deny her?

"It's all right by me." I smile.

"Thank you, Killian." She smiles in my direction.

* * *

"How did you find Gerald? I know he can be a lot to handle sometimes." We walk back to the palace after our little stroll around the grounds. The stroll was quiet, apart from the small chitchat we had.

"I thought he was sweet."

"Sweet?" I ask, curious.

"Yeah, he's willing to help me find justice, and I can see how much he cares about you." She smiles.

"He's been there for most of my life, I honestly don't know what I would do without him." It's true, I really don't. He's the main reason I haven't failed at being Lord. He helped me get through the grief of my parents' deaths and the lack of a bond with Dorian.

"Well, I'm glad you have someone like that. It must be nice." Such sadness in her tone, I hate that for her.

"I'm sorry," I apologize, not even sure why.

# Chapter Thirty-One

It's been two days since I met Gerald and he promised to help me solve the case of my mother's murder, but I haven't seen him since. I guess it doesn't have to happen straightaway, but I just assumed it would.

"Zillard for your thoughts?" Killian comes up to stand beside me.

"I haven't seen Gerald; do you know where he is?"

"I had to send him to Air Court for some business, I didn't know you wanted to see him today." There's a slight annoyance in his tone.

"Of course, don't you remember his promise to me?" My tone is sharp with annoyance. How could he forget?

"Ah, yes. Look, I don't know when he will get to it, his priority is me." Killan avoids my glaring gaze.

"I thought he is ours, Killian, isn't that the whole point in becoming a Lady of this court? Sharing subjects, doing everything together, and ruling Fire Court." I turn around to face him, throwing his words back at him. I know that is selfish of me but I'm stating facts.

"He isn't some kind of plaything, Aisling." He says my name with such venom. What has gotten into him?

"I have to go, there's a meeting I must attend." Killian turns to leave, but I reach out and grab his arm.

"Shouldn't I attend this meeting as well?" I ask.

"No. Go do something else, I'm sure the market will suit your time better." He pulls his arm out of my grasp.

I'm shocked, defeated, and slightly embarrassed with how he just spoke to me. It's like I mean nothing to him, just a *trophy wife*. Argh, I groan.

I stalk off to *his* bedroom, I want to fit into the villages, but I know I shouldn't standout and draw attention to myself.

* * *

The village market is nothing like I've seen before, sure Water Court has them but nothing to this extent. There are so many stalls with beautiful rugs, dresses, jewelry, food, and much more. Since the ball will be soon, I think maybe a piece of jewelry would be beautiful to have. Maybe I could even dress around it.

I walk past stunning stalls, smelling the different food aromas, and children playing chasey in the middle of the walkway.

"Can I help you, dear?" an elderly lady speaks up from behind a fabric stall.

"No, thank you, I'm just browsing." I touch the hanging fabrics, all range in different colors and textures. The gold, purple, light blue, and a sparkling pink stand out amongst the other colors they have on display. I continue down the pathway and spot an elegant jewelry stall. I walk over to it and my eyes have never seen so many beautiful jewels.

"A special occasion, dear?" the little old lady asks me. She's a lot shorter than me but built strong. I bet she has a lot of stories to tell. I wonder if I'll ever get to hear of how these people live, what they've been through and their challenges.

"Yes, actually, I'm not sure if you've heard that Lord Killian is hosting a ball at the end of the week." I'm trying not to give away who I am.

"Everyone has heard about it, dear; the entire village is buzzing. We want to know what the occasion is. The Lord isn't known for his kindness around here." I'm taken aback by her words.

Not kind?

Who is he really then?

I'm lost in thought about Killian when I feel the same magic pulse in my veins again.

I turn around to see no one standing behind me, I can't explain the feeling but it's like I am charged with magic. I feel much more powerful than what I am.

Not sure where I'm going, I leave the little old lady and start walking toward the pull of magic.

The pull takes me away from the market completely and toward abandoned homes. I'm starting to feel scared, wary of where I am. It's not too late to turn around and ignore the pull.

"You found me, sweetheart." Dorian stands out from the shadows.

"What are you doing here?" I hiss at him.

"I wanted to have a moment with you, without eyes and ears." He takes a step toward me.

"I shouldn't be here." I take a step back, away from him.

My entire being is still zinging, my magic feels alive.

Could it be like this every time I'm around Dorian?

Can't be.

"You feel it too, don't you?"

"I don't know what you're talking about." I take another step back.

"Of course, you do, sweetheart. Otherwise, you wouldn't be here." He smirks as he takes a step toward me again.

I hold up my hand to stop him from getting closer. I can't believe what I'm hearing, but I know deep down that it's true.

"Why can't your brother find out about us knowing each other?" I ask him, needing to know why I'm such a secret.

"He doesn't like being second-best, especially with women. I thought it was the best option, and that way I can keep... *us* a secret longer." The way he says us makes my entire body shiver with possibilities.

"Only reason I'm here wandering the markets is because your brother won't bother to let me in on his meetings, nothing to do with you," I dig back.

"You walked ten minutes away from the market, you were following the magic pull. I did the same and it led me to you." Dorian smiles but I can see curiosity in his eyes. There's something about the way he looks. It's almost like he doesn't believe it either.

"I can't explain it," I say quieter than a whisper.

"Neither can I..." He holds out his palm, waiting for me to take it.

I hesitate and decide I should take the leap.

My hand touches his soft skin and everything around us brightens and images float around our heads. Happy images, ones we've shared, ones we are yet to share. I can't believe what I'm seeing. All the images are surrounded in a purple hue.

"What... what is happening?" I ask.

"I don't know," Dorian answers me. His face shows disbelief, like he can't believe what's happening here.

I take my hand off his and the images disappear.

"Should we try that again?" he suggests,

"I'm not sure if we should."

"Don't you want to know?"

"I do, but is it going to be like that every time we touch?"

"So, you're saying there is a next time?" He winks at me.

"Let's get this over with." I place my hand down on his palm again and nothing. Nothing happens, no flash of light, no images. Nothing.

"Is it a one-time thing?" I ask, thinking he knows the answer.

"I don't know, did that happen with you and Killian?"

"No... I've never experienced that before, only with you." The surprise on his face is evident.

"What about you?"

"Nothing, never." I'm surprised. This is all overwhelming. I have to get back to the palace, I'm sure Killian is looking for me.

"I have to go..." I start to turn around, but Dorian grabs on to my arm.

"I want to give you this, it was my mother's and I know it'll look great on you." He reaches into his pocket and pulls out a necklace. It's gold, with tiny purple stones lining the chain, and in the middle is a large amethyst gemstone. It's beautiful.

"I can't take this; you shouldn't be giving me jewelry, Dorian!" I snap. What would his brother think?

"Say it's a wedding gift, and Killian hasn't seen this necklace before. He was too busy pleasing Father to notice our mother." Dorian spits the word *father*.

"I'm sorry." I take the necklace from his hand and put it in my bag.

I suppose I could wear it to the ball, but I need a dress to go with it.

# Chapter Thirty-Two

"Hold still, please." I start to fidget; I've been standing in the same spot for over four hours. I didn't think getting fitted for a gown would be this painful.

"I am," I groan out.

"Are we nearly done?"

"Yes, we are, please be patient. Don't you want this dress to be amazing?" one of my ladies asks me.

"Of course I do, but I need to go to the toilet and I'm hungry," I whine.

"A Lady of Fire Court would never complain," another one of my ladies comments.

"Luckily, I don't have that title... yet," I retort.

"Are you sure you want this color?" I am asked, with a hint of disgust.

I've chosen a deep purple hue with slight blue wisps at the bottom of the hem. It'll go perfectly with the necklace Dorian gave me.

"A red dress would be expected of you to represent this Court."

"That's exactly why I haven't chosen that color, it's not me. When I become the Lady of Fire Court, that is when my color palette will change, but until then, I will wear whatever color I choose." I brace my shoulders, tilt my chin up, and end this conversation.

"Yes, My Lady," they all say in unison.

I want to change the subject but I'm not sure how to, my mind keeps wanting to know about Gerald. Is he back yet?

Damn to hell I say.

"Is Gerald back yet?" I ask no one in particular.

"No, but we were instructed to give you this letter only if you asked for him." The smallest of the lady's maids walks over to the desk in the corner of the room, pulls open one of the tiny drawers, and pulls a letter from it.

She walks over this way and hands it to me.

It has my name written neatly on the front; I carefully open it.

Aisling,

I apologize that I couldn't make our meeting today. Killian has extended my stay. I have sent several documents I have obtained from Water Court to help you with your research about your mother.

I hope it helps.

Until next time.

Gerald.

I wonder how he gathered these notes from Water Court, it wouldn't have been easy to do so.

* * *

Later that afternoon, I'm thinking about the documents Gerald gave me and how redacted they are. How did he think I would be able to read them? I wonder if there's any way we could try and make sense of them.

I feel my eyes start to droop, feeling my body start to relax, I drift off to sleep.

Dreamland...


*"Hello, Sweetheart." I whirl around and spot Dorian leaning against my doorframe.*

*"What are you doing here?" I ask him. What if Killian spots us?*

*"Relax, it's your dream." He smirks at me.*

*"Oh." I shuffle my feet until the back of my knees hits the back of the bed. I sit down and place my hands in my lap.*

*"I didn't think I was going to get another visit from you."*

*"I'm sorry, I've been a bit busy... Killian has me doing official Court duties before I head back to my post." He stares at me, trailing his eyes from mine down to my neck, my chest, and all the way down to my toes. My entire body is electrified.*

*"I have so many questions..." I trail off, not sure where to even begin.*

*"I'm not sure I'm the person who can answer them, I do know whatever this..." He gestures between us with his hand. "Is nothing I have ever experienced before, and I haven't even had you yet." My cheeks heat with his intense words.*

*"I mean..." I shrug. "There was that one dream we shared that felt real." I avoid his eyes, my cheeks remaining heated.*

*"That was only a fantasy, Ash... when I take you, it will be so real you'll never want to dream again." His words... how can he say such intense things to me?*

*"Is there something between us?" I just have to ask.*

*He just smiles at me as I feel my body shaking and the dream world starting to fade.*


I groan.

"Why?" I say to whoever woke me.

"It's time to start getting ready for the ball." I groan again. I would much rather have stayed in my dream than attend a political ball with a guy I have no interest in marrying, but I will do so because I prefer to keep my head.

# Chapter Thirty-Three

It's been a few days since the ball, and I don't know how to begin to describe my thoughts about it. I did enjoy myself, but I also felt out of place... like I didn't belong there. It wasn't my place, I wouldn't exactly say I didn't feel safe, but I had that urge to keep looking over my shoulder. Almost like there was danger nearby... lurking... waiting.

My power was on edge, it felt threatened, but it felt different, like it was growing... changing.

The night was... intense, to say the least.

My sensitive ears hear the echoes of heavy boots running on the ground away from my room. I don't think I've heard anyone running in this court.

Is something happening?

I march over to my wardrobe and throw my gown over my head, needing it off before I put my fighting leathers on, if there is something serious happening, I need to be prepared. I reach into my overnight bag I keep under the bed and gather up my daggers. I knew one day I would need them again. I place them in their holders, standing straight and glancing at myself in the mirror.

This... this is who I'm supposed to be.

A warrior.

I open the bedroom door but am immediately pushed back in.

"What the..." I trail off.

"Shhh," the intruder says quietly.

I take a step back, hands hovering over my daggers.

"You don't need them, and you can always use your power." I know that voice, the person standing in front of me removes the hood and I don't believe my eyes.

"Hi, Ash." Neeshah is standing in the flesh right in front of me.

I shut the door behind her and usher her more into the room.

I don't believe it.

"What are you doing here?" I ask her.

"I needed to see you, I have so much to tell you, but I knew leaving a letter wouldn't be wise." She starts to pace the room.

"What is going on?"

"Well, you know there is a threat... otherwise—" She gestures to my fighting leathers. "You wouldn't be in those..." I look down at my clothes. She is right.

"But that doesn't explain what *you* are doing here?"

"I'm from Fire Court, remember?"

"Yes, of course I do, but that doesn't explain why you didn't graduate the Academy. Where have you been?" I haven't seen her since that night she almost... well, she did threaten the teachers to try and find Micka.

"I don't have much time, there's going to be an attack

here. I need you to go somewhere safe. They won't hurt you; I've given them orders not to." Orders?

"What are you talking about? What have you gotten yourself into, Neesh?" I take a step forward.

"It's best we have a short amount of time together. Just don't trust anyone, okay... not until I come get you." She starts to walk away from me, but I grab her wrist to stop her from exiting the door.

"I need more than that."

"I can't, not right now. You just have to trust me." With that, she pulls her hood on over her head. I let go of her wrist and she exits my bedroom.

What is going on?

Stay safe?

She will come for me.

Don't trust anyone... except her...

Left standing here, alone in my bedroom stewing over her words, I decide to take action. I need to find Killian and get him to put me on patrol... at least in Fire Court, this house.

I follow the sounds of the marching footsteps and I see Killian standing next to Dorian, deep in conversation.

"I want to be put to use," I demand once I stand in the middle of both of them. Their eyes shoot to mine once I open my mouth.

"No," they say in unison.

"I'm sorry, I didn't ask for permission. It was a demand." I cross my arms over my chest, trying to keep my power at bay. It can be unpredictable when I'm angry.

"It's too dangerous for you, I won't allow it."

"Why? Because I'm to be your bride?" I turn to Killian.

"Yes, that's exactly the reason." I huff.

"I have been trained for this purpose! I want to fight; I am ready to fight."

"Let me handle this." Dorian reaches out and places his hand on his brother's shoulder. Instantly he calms down.

"Come with me!" Dorian drops his hand and reaches for mine; he tugs me to follow him.

We find a small gap in the corridor between two pillars.

"Are you trying to get yourself killed?" Dorian hangs his head low, his lips so close to mine I can feel his breath on my cheeks.

"No," I breathe out. "I want to help; I was trained to do exactly this."

"Trained, yes, but you are not ready. No one is ever ready for the fight of their lives." He sighs.

"It's a lot worse than what it is here. Earth Court's outpost has been attacked." My breath hitches.

Earth Court, outpost... that's where my brother is!

"Before you get any crazy ideas, I'm heading there now. You must stay here. This court is the safest of them all." He lifts his head to finally meet my gaze.

"My brother..."

"I know, that's why I need you here. Safe. I will come back for you." His eyes flicker to my lips and back to mine, silently asking for permission.

I nod and close my eyes for the impact this is going to leave on my soul.

His soft lips touch mine, the kiss started out slow and gentle until we both became needy for each other.

We break apart, both breathless.

"I have to go; I will come back for you." He touches his lips against mine in the softest kiss again.

I close my eyes, not wanting to see him walk away from me.

A moment later, I open them back up and he's gone.

What am I going to do?

Follow this man into war or listen to him and remain here... safe?

# Chapter Thirty-Four

I remained in Fire Court a mere twenty-four hours.

The most painful day of my life. I knew I wouldn't remain here to be safe like some kind of pet.

I am a warrior and I need to start acting like one.

There are guards stationed outside my bedroom door, making sure no one can enter beside Killian himself... But I know the real reason for them being there, it's to keep me inside. Away from everything... safe.

Well, fuck being safe.

I am going to fight this war!

I pace back and forth in the bedroom, thinking of ways to try and escape. To at least make it down to Earth Court. I need to be with my brother, then my thoughts start to shift to Aylee and Josh. I wonder where they have been stationed. I haven't heard a word from them since leaving the Academy. What if they are both at Earth Court as well?

I can't just stay here and be Killian's pet.

I will not allow it!

The rage burning inside me sparks something.

My entire body is engulfed in flames.

I internally scream, but it doesn't last.

The flames aren't burning my skin, it's almost like that time when Neeshah was using her flames.

Her power is fire.

Could this mean?

No.

Can't be...

Do I have the ability to use fire?

**You've finally lured fire, Special One.**

The voice filters through my mind.

*That can't be right,* I say back in my head. *I'm a Water Fae.*

**Oh, Special One, you are more than just a Water Fae.**

I inhale a sharp breath at the statement. I know deep down in my bones that it's true. I am more than just a Water Fae.

If I can now control fire, I wonder what type of abilities I'm able to conjure up.

**Test it out...**

The voice whispers through my mind.

I close my eyes and think about how I will be able to get to Dorian in time. I know a horse is fast but is it fast enough?

All of a sudden, I open my eyes and everything around me is dark but sparkling. I reach out but my hands come up empty and it just disappears.

I'm not standing on the opposite side of the bedroom.

How?

How did that happen?

Wait... did time and space stop around me.

Can I actually teleport?

**I believe you can, Special One**

Holy shit.

This can't be real.

Let's see if I can do it again, maybe it was a one-time offer.

I close my eyes, think of the space between me and where I want to go next. I think of the only quiet place in this palace and my entire body morphs into time and space again. I can feel the everything and nothingness all at once.

My eyes open and sure enough, I'm in the library. I hope you don't need to envision the destination to transport somewhere. I wonder if I can think of a person, and I can just be there... with them.

I quickly avert my thoughts; I need my backpack before I can even try to attempt to get to Dorian and my brother.

My body is back in my bedroom, I gather the backpack and make quick work of getting it packed with my essentials.

I take a deep breath, close my eyes, and picture Dorian.

His perfect smile, those brooding eyes, and that curly but soft hair I'm dying to wrap my fingers in.

In a blink of an eye, the space between standing in my bedroom and being outside is incredible.

But what I find more incredible, I haven't gotten motion sickness yet.

Oh, wait.

My stomach tightens, my throat swells, and whatever I ate this morning is now on the ground at my boots.

"Ash?" I hear a male voice behind me.

I quickly wipe my mouth and turn around.

Expecting to see either Dorian or my brother standing behind me, who I find shocks me to my core.

"Josh?"

"What are you doing here? Last I heard you are supposed to be in Fire Court." He takes a step toward me.

"Well, I'm here." I shrug casually.

"Where's Aylee?" I ask him, looking around the campsite. All I see are men walking around, talking, and laughing with each other.

"She's not here."

"What do you mean she isn't here? Shouldn't she be here with you?" I thought they would have gotten stationed together.

"She's north, in Air Court."

"What?" I say in shock.

"They don't know we have bonded... otherwise, we are a threat and we decided to keep that to ourselves. It's painful being away from your mate, but we manage. We get some leave to meet each other but now that we've been under attack, it's going to be a bit harder now."

"Fuck," I say, I had no idea.

"I'll ask again, what are you doing here, Ash?" Josh's tone isn't playful anymore, he almost sounds hurt, angry.

"I've come to do my duty." I tilt my chin up.

"Your duty was to stay in Fire Court!" Oh shit.

I turn around and now I'm standing in front of Dorian.

"I thought you would have been happy to see me, at least."

"Happy? No. Angry. Yes. What the fuck, Ash!" He takes a step forward.

"I want to be here!" I yell, I feel the flames lick out of my fingers and caress my palms. Dorian follows my line of sight, and he inhales a sharp breath.

"Ash?" he asks.

"Oh, this?" I move my hands through the air, showing off my new power.

"I discovered it back in Fire Court. I'm just as shocked as you are." I smile. This new power is everything. I feel more alive, more alert than ever before.

The fire disappears when Dorian closes the distance between us.

"Ash..." He reaches forward with his hand, tilting my chin to look up at him.

"Your brother..." He trails off.

"What about my brother? He is the next person I want to see." The excitement I feel when I'm so close to seeing him again is overwhelming.

"He's badly hurt, he's in the infirmary." Dorian's gaze never leaves mine.

"I have to go see him!" I demand.

"You can't... he's with the healers right now. The best place for you right now is in my tent, away from the danger." I groan. Of course, he would say that.

"I just got word, there is a fleet that will be on our shoreline by the morning."

"So, we only have tonight? Could this be our only night together?" I place my hand on Dorian's chest.

"Yes." His voice sad with the realization.

"Then let's make it real and not in some dream..." I trail off.

"Let's take a bath." I follow Dorian back to his tent. I know he would have wards in place for people to not enter, or he will be alerted by their presence.

There's nothing I can do about my brother, and I know Josh is one hell of a fighter. I will worry about them both tomorrow when I'm standing shoulder to shoulder with them for when the enemy arrives, but for tonight.

I will soak in everything that Dorian has to offer.

# Chapter Thirty-Five

Dorian's tent is magnificent. He's definitely used magic to make it more homey than any other tent outside.

"The bath is over there." He points in the far corner of the room, it's an open tent, the bed is in the middle of the room, the bath is in the far right of the corner and the far left has a desk with stacks of paper on it, with trays of food. Untouched.

I walk to the bath and undress.

My feet slip into the water, and I sit down, letting the water engulf me.

"Will you join me?" I ask Dorian.

"I would rather wash you first instead, if that's okay." I nod.

Dorian smiles, closes the space between us, picks up the washcloth, dips it into the water, and then proceeds to wash my arms, one at a time. He glides the cloth down my chest, over the rounds of my breasts and down to my stomach. He pauses for a moment, looking at me for guidance of whether he should continue. I nod.

Dorian makes a slow trail down my stomach to the softness between my legs, he hovers there for a second before moving the washcloth down both of my legs. I can feel the heat in my cheeks. I haven't been with anyone who was this gentle, this loving, or anyone who took their time with *me*.

"You're blushing, Aisling, am I doing something you like?" Dorian speaks in a playful tone.

"I am not blushing." I quickly turn my face away from him to hide the little half smile that's plastered on my lips.

He splashes some water on my face, and I turn around in shock.

"As if you did that!" I splash water back at him.

"Oh, it's on..." He is forgetting that I am a Water Fae... and I never play fair.

I look him dead in the eyes and smirk. I can feel the tingling pulse within my blood whenever I conjure my water element. I close my eyes and imagine a scene of water, whether it be a tidal wave or shapes of animals made from water, but this time I use tiny droplets. I form them like rain and make them land on top of his head.

He laughs, like a deep belly laugh, when he is drenched in water.

"No, you don't play fair!"

He stands up and hauls me out of the bath. I squeal with a picture of delight and terror, wondering what this man is doing to me.

He tosses me over his shoulder, completely butt naked, and then places me on the bed.

He leans over me, one hand on either side of my head. I meet his eyes, my heart fluttering in my chest like a bird trapped in a cage.

I never thought our first time would be during our last night before war breaks out, but here we are.

His eyes are dark and smoldering, causing my stomach to flutter. The mood dampens for a split second when I can see the wheels turning in his head, as if he just came to the same realization I did.

Finally, he leans down, brushing his nose along my cheek. "No," he decides, saying out loud that tomorrow's problems won't ruin this mood. Dorian presses a lingering kiss to my forehead, causing me to melt.

He brushes a strand of hair out of my face, his eyes darkening from the electricity between us.

"Are you ready for this time to be real?" Dorian asks me.

I can only manage to nod my head. He's made me speechless.

Dorian leans closer to me and places his lips against mine.

It's a soft and slow kiss at first, but the longing and need start to fill both of our bodies. I never thought this day would come, when we get to become one. Is it wrong of me that I was with Gerrick at the Academy or being promised to Killian? The only thought that matters in this moment is Dorian... but it's too late now, desire takes over.

I need to feel him, the need to feel his naked skin against mine is strong... and I need it now.

I feel his hands travel down my breasts, going over the curves of my hips. He slowly moves his hands down my thighs and back up again and stops just above my sex.

I'm naked and Dorian is still fully clothed.

"Your turn," I whisper against his lips.

He doesn't hesitate when he leans back for me to reach up and untie his leather jacket. Once that's off, I make quick work of his leather pants. He stands up off the bed and slowly takes them off. The suspense is killing me, but before I can say anything, I glance down and his rock-hard cock springs free and it just sits up against his stomach.

I swallow hard. I've never been with someone with such a large cock before. I yearn for his touch, now more than ever before.

Dorian just stands there, letting me soak him in. The large tent around him is making him seem small.

God, I love magic.

I swallow hard when my back hits the smooth sheets, my head now resting on the softest pillows I've ever lain on. Dorian slowly moves up the bed and is now towering over me. I want to feel his naked body against mine, so I reach up and pull him to me. I feel his hand move down my body, feeling his way to smooth sex, he continues going down south. He drags one finger over my clit and then he reaches its target... my center.

I hear Dorian hum with pleasure.

"Are you ready?" he asks me while positioning himself on top of me.

"Yes," I breathe.

Dorian thrusts into me and I gasp at how large he is.

After two slow and gentle thrusts, he starts to pick up his pace but not by much.

"Ash," Dorian groans.

It doesn't take long before he picks up the pace and his thrusts become more powerful.

This feeling is getting too much for me; I can feel my orgasm coming. Dorian knows that too, but he doesn't stop. He keeps going faster and harder until we are both shaking with pure joy.

I arch my back, my toes curling in the bedsheets, and I scream Dorian's name.

My whole body is still tingling when he finishes after

me. He leans down to kiss my forehead, and then he rolls onto his back but not too far away from me.

I move over to my side, and I rest my head on his chest.

"I can't believe we did that..." I trail off, exhausted and out of breath.

"Was it better than your dream?" he asks me.

"Oh, so much better, better than I could have even imagined." I smile into his chest.

"What are we going to do?" I can't help but ask him.

"What do you mean?"

"With everything... Killian... the war... my brother?" There is so much uncertainty right now that I think my head might explode.

"I'll take care of my brother; the war is nothing new... and your brother will make a full recovery." I nod. I know he is right.

"Sleep, that can be all sorted and discussed tomorrow." Dorian leans down and kisses my head. I know it is, but I can't help it...

I start to feel my eyes to shut and complete darkness sweeps me away.


I wake in the middle of the night, sweat running down my face, my entire body covered in sweat.

What is going on?

Maybe it's the impending doom that's to come with the sunrise, but this feels different.

**Come to the water, Special One**

The voice, it's beckoning me to leave the tent, leave Dorian.

I'm dressed only in a white sleeping dress. I slip on my

boots, turn to see Dorian still fast asleep, and slip out of the tent.

I walk through the campsite, there is no one around except for the odd soldier doing a patrol. I hope I don't run into anyone while I'm out. Dressed like this is bad for my image.

My feet touch the sand crunching under my boots and once my eyes lock onto the water, I feel home.

At peace...


DORIAN


I wake with a jolt, I open my eyes and scan the bed, Ash isn't here.

Where could she have gone?

**Best hurry up, Warrior**

The voice... what is she doing?

I toss the blankets off my body, throw on my fighting leathers, and follow my instinct.

It's telling me to head for the water's edge.

**You're close, Warrior**. Ameria, my dragon says to me in my mind.

I never thought I would have bonded with a dragon, let alone *the* Guardian of our realm.

She's been informative with everything, except why the other lesser Guardians won't bond. She's kept that pretty private, and I knew not to overstep when she's huff and gruff about it. She is a hothead.

My steps are heavy, trying to get to the beach fast enough but when I step out from the shadows of the trees and see Aisling standing there, at the edge of the shoreline, my breath hitches.

Her white flowing dress blows around in the wind, her long hair swishing and swaying with the breeze, but yet I don't feel any wind...

I see her extend her neck up to the sky and that's when I see it...

I see her...

Ameria.

Her wings flapping in the sky, barely visible to make out that it is her.

I slowly step toward Ash, knowing she hasn't seen a dragon before, but only read about them in books, ancient books.

"Ash!" I call out, but she barely moves, giving me the confirmation that she hasn't heard me.

I take another step forward, but before I can call out her name again...

She just vanishes.

"Dorian!" I hear her yell my name, but it isn't out loud or an echo.

It is in my mind.


To be continued

EVAGONN

REALM

DRAGON
KEEP

ISLE OF
FATES

Guardian
Keep

PHOENIX

SERPANT

PRIMTHOD

Stardiana • NIGHT
COURT

DUSK
COURT • Valtiria

Dilchburg •

DAWN
COURT

Sunniris • DAY
COURT

Utrnia
Outpost

ISLE OF
PROMISE

Ebonvaler

AR

G

AMAROK
NIXIAM
WALDARIE
ISLE OF MYXIE
VARDI PRISON
Bloomsbury
Hesradia
SPRING COURT
SUMMER COURT
Oranlinvale
LOGOXDIN
AUTUMN COURT
WINTER COURT
Blizzville
VARDIRIAN
EDOX
OUROBOROS
N
W
E
S

# Acknowledgments

If you've made it this far, thank you.

Thank you for taking the time out of your busy lives to read this book and that I can share my amazing world with you all.

This is my first time writing a fantasy novel. I thought it would have been easy since I've written a few books, but I was knocked for a six.

Fantasy isn't easy to write, I take my hat off to those who write it for a living.

I enjoyed creating this world, and the tie-in worlds to come but shh....

Tom & EJ, thank you for allowing me the time to write, to enjoy my characters and their world.

Tom, thanks for letting me rant on about the connections that I had to make, for the characters to make sense and the endless plot holes I created and needed to fix.

EJ, for being my cutest little man. Mummy loves you.

I love you both fiercely.

Mum and Emma, thank you for your endless support in my passion to create stories.

Beta Babes, Michelle, Anastasia, Lauren, Phylicia & Maddison.

My amazing editor Karen, thank you for putting up with me for all these years.

To the readers, thank you for still believing in me and taking the chance on this story.

# About the Author

Hi!

I am Chloe but my pen name is Chloe O'Connor.

I have loved books since I was little. My journey started with reading the fairy tales we grew up with, to the worlds of fantasy as we got older.

Now, I have dived into creating my own worlds with characters you love, love to hate, and villains we secretly crave.

From dragons to Fae wielding the elements mixed with a little spice, you can't really go wrong!

If you like suspense, historical, murder mystery, contemporary, or psychological thriller, then check out my other pen name ... C. Renee

Please stay in touch at: LINKTREE

This is where you'll be able to find my other titles from both Chloe O'Connor & my other pen name C. Renee.